Seeing Further

T0262402

Seeing Further

ESTHER KINSKY

Translated from the German by Caroline Schmidt

nyrb **New York Review Books** New York

This is a New York Review Book
published by The New York Review of Books
207 East 32nd Street, New York, NY 10016
www.nyrb.com

The translation of this work was supported in part by a grant from the Goethe-Institut.

Library of Congress Cataloging-in-Publication Data
Names: Kinsky, Esther, author. | Schmidt, Caroline, translator.
Title: Seeing further / by Esther Kinsky; translated by Caroline Schmidt.
Other titles: Weiter sehen. English
Description: New York: New York Review Books, 2024.
Identifiers: LCCN 2024006514 (print) | LCCN 2024006515 (ebook) |
  ISBN 9781681378510 (paperback) | ISBN 9781681378527 (ebook)
Subjects: LCSH: Kinsky, Esther—Fiction. | LCGFT: Autobiographical fiction. |
  Novels.
Classification: LCC PT2711.I67 W4513 2024 (print) | LCC PT2711.I67
  (ebook) | DDC 833/.92—dc23/eng/20240216
LC record available at https://lccn.loc.gov/2024006514
LC ebook record available at https://lccn.loc.gov/2024006515

ISBN 978-1-68137-851-0
Available as an electronic book; ISBN 978-1-68137-852-7

Printed in the United States of America on acid-free paper.

10 9 8 7 6 5 4 3 2 1

Contents

In memory of Martin Chalmers
my cinema man from Glasgow
who walked with me and was my guide

There is something important in people, something that's dying—the senses, a universal thing. We can't agree on politics, but maybe we can agree on senses. We are dying of sadness. The whole world is dying of sadness. We are the enemy.

—John Cassavetes

I. Prelude

I spy, I spy with my little eye

YEARS AGO, I was sitting on a bench by a fjord in Norway, far up north. The landscape was dramatic: craggy mountains, dark water, every so often rippled by a gust of wind. Spring had arrived early, bringing the snow to melt under a pale sun. In the unexpected light of that Sunday afternoon a number of people from the nearby university town had set out on foot for a short excursion. They passed by on the path behind the bench, remnant snow crunching beneath their soles, conversing in calm tones, some with muffled laughter; there was something ceremonious about this procession of walkers and, for a moment, without turning around, I imagined I sat with my back to a film by Carl Theodor Dreyer.

A woman joined me on the bench. She appeared as un-Norwegian as I felt myself to be. She was short and plump and, in my memory, she was swinging her legs. For a while we both looked at the dark fjord and then in English she asked where I was from. She herself had fled the war in her native Yugoslavia a few years earlier, and after a prolonged search found a position at the university in the nearby town. She told me about the war and the region from which she came, the flatlands of northern Serbia, a town not far from the Hungarian border. She described the river, the large cornfields and the composition of the cities and villages, where all the roads were laid out as if drawn with a ruler, running ramrod straight from south to north or east to west, and, because the region was very flat, in many places you could see from one end of a street to the other and even farther, to the horizon. As the Norwegian spring day reached its end and her teeth began to chatter from the cold, she expanded on the flatness and vastness of her southern, dusty native district, which in light of our surroundings seemed virtually unimaginable and downright fabulous, and lastly she mentioned that there, in this landscape which had once been part of Hungary and in spirit was still aligned with the Hungarian capital, even though a border now separated it from former Yugoslavia, they said you only needed to climb on a pumpkin to be able to see all the way to Budapest. Imagine that, she said, shivering, just imagine it: You climbed on a pumpkin and up there you could see further, on and on and on.

II.

It is seeing which establishes our place
in the surrounding world.
—JOHN BERGER, *Ways of Seeing*

WHERE TO DIRECT the gaze?
There are two aspects of seeing: *what* you see and *how* you see it.
This investigation into *seeing further* will involve only the question
how. It pertains to the place that the viewer takes. It concerns point
of view and remove from the things and images, from the action,
proximity and distance, vastness. Vastness is more than physical; it
is the scope of possibilities you allow. This applies to looking at a
landscape, a terrain, at people, at art. In the past century no location
was as important for the *how* of seeing, for contemplating the place
that a viewer assigns themself or takes, as the cinema—as a venue,
as a space. This space, whose relevance and significance did not even
withstand a century, has been closing ever further in recent decades.
The view out of the dark into a vastness created by film grows narrower as this venue for seeing disappears. The collective experience
facilitated by this space is disappearing along with it, as is the more-
or-less emphatic joy of taking part in these experiential possibilities,
and this loss, whether mourned or not, deserves to be described and
merits consideration. The cinema was the stage of a century. Today

people differ in their relationship to this venue. Why the cinema? After all, films are available in other formats; the black box of the auditorium is considered a necessary venue for seeing by only few, and some even brush off the cinematic experience as an elitist pastime. As if the only thing that mattered any more was the *what*. And no longer the *how*.

Despite being relegated to the fringes of the action, the cinema still retains some mythic quality as a venue for seeing. The more the privatization of all experience eats away at our lives, the more fabulous appears a venue where seeing was a collective experience, where wit, terror, dismay and relief found a communal expression without encroaching on the anonymity afforded by the dark room. Even those who never visit the cinema any more will still remember particulars of the experience, of the place; the act of entering into the dark in order to then look out of it; the unspoken, abided by rule of seeing: "All eyes in the same direction." In the direction mastered by the projectionist, invisible to the audience.

Seeing is a proficiency you acquire. A competence you slowly become aware of. Should you desire. In the beginning there is always the framed view. From the inside to the outside, from a window, whose cutout determines the world for the person looking out. Then comes a discovery: the discrepancy between the way things look from the window and the way they look when you are outside, surrounded by an unframed world, your eye itself now part of the world. A child's view from the window into a winter morning of hoarfrost

4

and fog remains engraved in the mind as a promise and a mystery; from the garden path or the roadside that same overgrown, rimy terrain rouses confusion, becomes branded in the mind as a memory of the world's strangeness, which needs sizing up. A winter morning as the first film: a montage from various angles and perspectives. Visiting each window in the house on a quest to watch the outside transform into a series of cutouts which the contemplating eye alone can read and fill with narrative, whereas outside those same things, relinquished from their frames, become landmarks which the eye's corresponding self uses to determine their place in that outside. Out there you stood in the world and looked around as far as you could see, the eye always searching for a place to rest, whereas inside, standing by the window, you gazed at a framed fragment which could be ascribed or denied an absolute significance.

Later: binoculars. A new frame, a new, magical metamorphosis via manipulated distances. A fetched piece of yonder, transformed by the frame into a foreign land, into a fiction entirely liberated from its surroundings: The other side of the river, accessed in life outdoors only by crossing a bridge found farther upstream, became available as a result of the binoculars and the view was made obtainable, offering itself up to be filled with ideas entirely unrelated to the vague, blurry contours recognizable to the naked eye, embedded in the familiar gradation of fields, trolley embankment, waterside trees and a notion of the river. Seeing became an adventure, each look through the binoculars was a journey of discovery.

From binoculars to the camera viewfinder. As a child I received a small Russian camera with an inscription in Cyrillic letters. The camera was black and silver, girdled by a brown leather case that snapped onto it, with a protruding part, which could be folded down, covering the lens. The world was reflected on the surface of the lens, distorted to the point of unrecognition, and thanks to a mysterious technical correlation when I looked through the square viewfinder I saw what the eye of the lens saw. Suddenly the world could be divided into pieces, into fragments that became separate entities if you stared long enough through the viewfinder, and even more so later, once the fragments were spread out on the table as photographs and all memory of what had once surrounded these images receded into the shadows. What had been all around could then be reported, related, invented in words; it was excluded from the image. That was a revelation to me. The act of seeing, much more *how* to look than *what* to see, had become a decision.

One spring they destroyed the wild terrain across the street, which had always been the first thing I saw out my window every morning. Abandoned land, as they called it, *orphaned* land; the missing owners' heirs never turned up, the wilderness became land to build on, and in the morning my gaze now fell upon a construction site, piles of soil and trucks, later the skeleton of a multi-storey house, an apartment building. An act of violence was committed against the view; there was no further, there was no yonder any more, no mystery, and in winter no forms enchanted by hoarfrost. Families moved in, children who went to my school, and one day I stood on one of those balconies visible from my window, and looked down at my own house, at my own window. From the perspective of this newly built balcony, the spot from which I examined my world now appeared distressingly strange and distant; the window looked so small I couldn't believe it capable of the relevance it held for my seeing, for my preoccupation with the cutout of the world that it delineated. For the first time a question began to stir in me, unarticulated yet, about the relationship between seeing and being seen, about the mysterious connection between looking and being looked at. But I also saw past my house, out to the terrain leading to the river, which I was otherwise familiar with only from a different window found on the backside of my house, framed as if cut out from a larger whole. I saw the strips of field, the railroad embankment, the pikes of the poplar trees that lined both sides of the river, the factory behind the damp alluvial meadows with the 'migrant-worker shanties'; I saw further, all the way to the range of hills, bluish green and out of focus beyond the river, and down to the river bend country shimmering in whitish light, where the landscape flattened and dissolved into everything possible. This panorama of vague things, of vastness, of eventualities and all the stories the river bend might have opened up into, remained for me a promise that oddly belonged to the cinema—as if this were the place where the worlds that I peered into from the darkness of the auditorium grew.

The cinema was not an everyday experience in my childhood. I grew up in a suburb, without a television, in fact, yet not close enough to a cinema for regular weekend visits. From time to time a theatre on wheels came along, set up a projector in a gymnasium, and there was a programme. Charlie Chaplin or, less frequently, Buster Keaton, with his absurdity pushing into chaos, as well as nature documentaries and animated films. Because of my nearsightedness I had to sit in one of the front rows, and for weeks I lost sleep over *Bambi*, those rolling eyes and the animals' distorted proportions. The cinema was better with 'real movies', for instance *Nils Holgerssons underbara resa*, even if the end was always difficult to bear. Not because of the story itself, but simply because the film had to end, because you couldn't go on watching, because the view out the window of the screen into another world had to close. Later my father occasionally took my siblings and me along to a cinema near a train station, where a main feature and an opening short and the weekly newsreel ran in an endless loop. You could join the sparse audience at any point, search for a seat in the dim glow of the usher's flashlight, and stay there. A cinema ticket meant you could spend the whole day, as some people liked to do on cold or wet days, and after the loop ran for the second time they were even tired enough to sleep. Many people smoked cigarettes; I remember plumes rising before the image and floating in the air. Most of the visitors clearly came to pass the waiting time at the train station; they carried small suitcases or valises, and once a man who sat in our row forgot his when he left the cinema hall in haste, rushing to catch his train or get to some appointment. I remember the musty smell of the cinema and the heavy, raw felt curtain through which you entered, the lower edges tipped in leather or synthetic leather dragging across the linoleum floor, and the usher, who had a curly head of hair and a tired face, who always tried to find us an empty row.

My father was a reticent man, and our trips to this cinema almost always transpired unannounced; later, if he had things to do, sometimes he would leave us alone there, and we wouldn't move an inch.

He never said a word about the films we saw, but at times I thought they might be messages, from the screen to him, or from him to us. In one film, for instance, a train crossed a tremendous prairie, heading towards pale, tall mountains in the distant background, approaching a village where, as the viewer already knew, several people were longingly awaiting its arrival at the station. I was sure it was a certain train in a region that our father had already told us about a few times—a scene from his childhood, for which the flatness of the landscape played a large role, since the trains were already recognizable on the horizon hours before they arrived. I never mentioned this connection, but I also didn't believe my father when he later explained to us that this scene was simulated with a toy train, since it wouldn't have been possible to film it otherwise, from so high up and with a view across such a tremendous landscape. If anything, an angel could do it, my brother said, an angel with wings. We all laughed at him for that. The idea of an angel with a movie camera.

These trips to the cinema under my father's supervision eventually came to an end, and a few years passed before the endless-loop cinema played a role in my life again. It was the rediscovery of a hot summer; I was a teenager, a child no longer, and one afternoon during break I was out roaming the streets alone, not knowing what to do with myself, when I suddenly stood in front of the cinema and it all came back. The programme had changed. There were no longer newsreels and no longer second- and third-rate facile films, arbitrarily selected for a tired audience to pass time with or perhaps even drift asleep to under the soporific influence of their predictability. Now they screened films whose titles sounded like something, which had distinction, a preceding ring. They weren't the latest films and there was still an occasional intermission, only now instead of newsreels there were advertisement breaks or short films, but the endless-loop concept remained unchanged. Something I had previously simply accepted—that you could enter at any time and stay seated for as long as you liked—now acted as a spell, which appeared to make room for the possibility of *luck*.

Under this spell the cinema was transformed from a refuge for shelter-seeking travellers on layovers into the preferred spot of a different crowd who sought to reach or come down from various states of intoxication, who came to enjoy and occasionally also sleep off a smoke-induced weightlessness. There were probably also quiet cinema lovers among them, visitors who simply sat in their seats and watched for as long as they could, and the scattered chroniclers, who in the weak glow of the emergency lights or standing next to the cracked foyer curtain would now and then scribble something into a notebook. All in all, things proceeded less noisily than before, although there were occasionally viewers who laughed to themselves, as if caught in a comical dream that had nothing to do with the film. I saw quite a few films in this cinema and for many of them I can still remember today the spot where I entered the auditorium and saw the first image on the screen. The last film I watched there was *Death in Venice*—nothing novel any more, but for me it remained distinctive, since a few years earlier, when I was still a child, in the milky light of northern Italy I stood on the sidelines among other curious spectators and watched the filming of a few scenes. The incongruence between my personal experience as a witness to a tiny, random phase in the metamorphosis of a vision into a film and the visible reality of that film on screen brought me to think about the

cinema again and again. It was not only the films that were important, but also the place itself. What unfurled on the projection screen
was invariably bound to this space, to the dark with a view into a
world, which despite being cropped always appeared larger than
your own, determined by other boundaries. Yet for all its vastness,
it was still bound to this physical place and determined by its features, all of which played a role: the way you entered the foyer
through a brown swinging door, traded a coin for an entrance ticket
made of rough paper, and dove through a bristly curtain into the
dark room; the smell of it; the moderately tiered seating rows with
strangers' skulls in silhouette, their hair variously coifed and styled.
Film wasn't a mere sequence of projected images—film was cinema,
and it became reality when the gaze met the screen, and the seeing
happened surrounded by other viewers. An experience unimaginable
without the presence of other participants, whose identities literally
remained in the dark although they were also silent confidants,
accomplices in seeing. And something took hold of me in there, in
this separate venue with invariably poor ventilation, something that
pointed the way and connected dots on the pale map of my minor
experiences such that an image emerged. A moving image with
blurred edges, which I never lost sight of.

A film on celluloid or 'cellulose acetate', the material later developed
for greater durability, is a peculiar creature. A compact, vulnerable
testimony to joint efforts, to interventions and encroachments, to
circumstances resulting from countless imponderable circumstances,
which at every showing technology and manual expertise help to
unfurl into a world capable of filling the dark watching room in

front of the screen so fully that reality outside the cinema, which proceeds according to the bidding of no recognizable entity, fades into the background for the length of time required by the strips of celluloid to travel at a fixed speed before a powerful light source, guided by several reels and spindles. In its density and absoluteness, for its viewers a film in the cinema is always a disruption in the course of the world. Countless people used to share the experience of this disruption without ever referring to it as such. It was a cultural fluency with its own small rituals, insiders, servants, artisans and henchmen, and then it began to crumble without relent. You could name the reasons why, but that wouldn't really help to understand the process. Of course the cinema isn't dead as long as there are still films whose ideal form, intended by all parties involved, is realized only when screened there. What *is* dead, however, is the compulsory communality of the cinematic experience that everyone agreed to, even if it is still preserved, beautiful and undecayed like Snow White, in some people's thoughts and memories, nourishing the fantasy of its reawakening. A dream in a glass coffin, set aside on some peripheral terrain. Even the seven dwarves are sitting at home by their screens, leaving the pallbearing to random romantics, undaunted volunteers, momentary hopefuls.

The cinema used to have presence, it had weight in almost everyone's life, not as an exceptional experience, but as a commonplace in a less privatized world that first the television invaded bit by bit, and later the permanent accessibility of private screens caused to fully unravel. In my old Russian and Polish language textbooks, the cinema played an even larger role than the factories, universities and outpatient clinics that also came up in many exercises. There was hardly a dialogue or a lesson in which the cinema was not visited, exited, missed or espoused under various grammatical pretences. Lands of promise, where the cinema determined life, spread out before my mind's eye. In my Polish textbook it was above all Cinema Wisła, which in the sketchy illustrations accompanying the exercises had a classical-seeming, nearly temple-like façade with small figures standing in front in little groups, the women wearing skirts that recalled the fashions of the fifties, the men in suits, and all of them carrying briefcases, to suggest that everyone had rushed directly from university, the outpatient clinic, or the factory to catch a film—because back then, when the cinema was still a part of life, it didn't matter if you were in Italy, France, Poland or the Federal Republic of Germany: the workers also carried briefcases, in which they stashed their snacks. Above or below the drawings there would be a dialogue, for instance: Do you already have plans for tonight?—Yes, I'm going to Cinema Wisła with Antek.—Oh, I'll come along! Or: Do you want to take a walk in Łazienki Park after the lecture?—No, I'm going to Cinema Wisła.

I took my first trip to Warsaw one September; the light was mild and grey-blue, the air scratched my throat and smelled of smoke, an odour that long remained characteristic of Eastern Europe. In the morning I walked over to the window in the apartment on Mickiewicza, in the Żoliborz district. The room was on the rear side of the apartment building, where there was a balcony full of potted geraniums, now gangly in autumn, a send-off to the dark time of year, and the first thing I saw past the flowers was the façade of Cinema Wisła. The lettering above the entrance looked exactly as it had in the textbook illustrations, reflecting the autumnal sunlight by day, and after nightfall the letters had a familiar glow, promising the fulfilment of expectations. My encounter with this cinema caught me off guard, and it remained as a backdrop of sorts in those weeks, when all of Warsaw appeared like a film. In the evenings when I walked past the cinema I noted that people without briefcases also went there, the men did not wear suits and the women were not in mid-calf-length skirts. I didn't see a film there myself, something kept me from doing so; maybe I was afraid if I climbed the steps the façade might reveal itself to be a cheap backdrop, and behind the entrance doors allotment gardens would open up, where weak fires smouldered and the last apples still hung from the trees, or a sea of rubble might spread out, with broken papier-mâché columns at first indistinguishable from real fragments of rubble weighing tons. But even without visiting the cinema I learned that Łazienki Park is located a fair distance from Cinema Wisła, at the opposite end of the city. Wisła is the Polish name for the Vistula River, which courses through Warsaw, grey-blue and murky from sand, and to my knowledge for a long time it remained the only river with a cinema named after it.

Where do they go in today's foreign-language textbooks? Are there still places of promise like Cinema Wisła, where the familiar—the cinema, purely and simply—mixes with the foreign, the unknown—the outpatient clinic, the factory, a river with a sonorous name—luring you into another language, which in turn opens up another world?

On my travels in Eastern Europe I looked for the cinema every new place I went. Practically every village had one, or had, after all, had one until the early nineties; the death of the cinema was learned from the West, where film became a private matter, where cinemas wasted away and eventually perished, while the few surviving films were distributed as luxury goods. The cinema as a classless place had died. The buildings of former cinemas were easy to recognize, their splendid traces still visible, along with, at times, a certain pride in their achievement, even if the cinema had not been in operation for some time. Market, cinema, cemetery: these were the three points of orientation in the places where I went. Eat, see, die. Or: See, eat, die. Those were the possible variations. Fewer and fewer cinemas were active but they were all still recognizable, closed and barricaded, but not yet repurposed or razed, occasionally painted with slogans or the names of football teams—decaying, decayed, but still there. These small temples entrusted to decay were found nearly everywhere, in Scotland and Sweden, in France and Italy. You hear of cinemas in train stations, where the locomotive whistles mixed with the films; of cinemas next to ringing cemetery chapels and the clubs of radical organizations; cinemas that provided stability and a home to the unhinged, to people suffering from dementia; and cinemas where dodgy business was done. The cinema was a place that fomented stories by robbing you of words before the screen, a place that has yet to find a replacement. These dormant motion-picture castles, with their worm-eaten, rusty, blockaded doors, remained standing as wonder walls, where you could not help but stop and consider how things should go on: with the act of looking. Where to direct the gaze?

In search of a view over the lowlands, on a hot day in May I left Budapest, heading for south-east Hungary. I wanted to see the plains, which I imagined being something like the Po Basin, shimmering in summer, often under a white, hazy sky, cloudless in this milky light. No one in Budapest had anything good to say about the flatland known as the Alföld; in a certain disparaging tone they told me there was not a single hill to be found between the small, gentle slope in Budapest City Park—which schoolchildren transformed into bare, dark, ploughed soil in less than fifteen minutes of sledding —and the tri-border area of Hungary, Serbia, and Romania; not a single hill, aside from the man-made river dykes, designed to prevent, or at least alleviate, flooding. Aside from a desire to see this flat country, I was drawn by a vague idea of boundlessness, the uniform light, and the suspension of temporality that occurs when there are few markers to designate spatial borders in the form of mountains, hills and large forests standing out against the sky. It was an artificial vision that dissolved past the Tisza River—into the vastness, shimmering with heat, the immense fields burgeoning with sunflowers and corn, the sparse acacia groves and the long, white, synthetic tunnels full of ripening watermelons—when I abandoned myself to seeing and nothing else, dropping every expectation. The distances between the villages increased, the roads grew emptier and bumpier, every movement outside stirred up clouds of dust, and a wall of dove-grey mist stood on the horizon. The Alföld was a landscape of emptiness, of repetition, of perplexingly similar names on town signs, a place of great slowness. Roaming dogs, cats slinking in the short midday shadows cast by yard gates and masonry walls, workers cycling past with three-tiered lunchboxes swaying on the handlebars of their bicycles, women in colourfully patterned smocks sweeping in front of the garden gates, everything moving in slow motion.

I had set out in the hope of taking photographs, yet out there in the daylight, which was blinding despite being clouded, I could hardly make out anything that yielded an image. Not a single piece allowed itself to be cut out of this vastness, this flatness and emptiness, without something entirely essential going missing in the image.

What was this essential quality that refused to submit to a frame? What cried 'invalid', whenever the square viewfinder closed around a cutout? I couldn't figure it out, and the more I saw the more it seemed outrageous to take a photograph that would cut a piece out of this landscape, comprised of only a small strip of earth below an immense sky, and declare it a whole.

I drove on slowly, without a plan or an aim, searching if anything for a point onto which I could fix my gaze. In a village I stopped at a tavern, where it reeked of old frying oil in the dark interior and hit songs played, and from a wide gallery that wrapped the room on three sides, creating an open second floor, men practised shooting. They had rifles pressed to their cheeks and they squinted, aiming at illuminated dots which moved slowly across screens. A muffled bang sounded regularly, followed by an exclamation I didn't understand, and sometimes a warbly whistling sound, to indicate which dot on the target was met. I left without ordering anything to eat, and in that short time the light outside had changed, or perhaps my gaze was different now, after having entered the dark bar-room; it had recovered from the glittering and was able to face the diffused light anew, postulating a haziness here, a blurring of the edges of shadows there. The wall on the south-western horizon appeared to have grown, a swelling of various blues ranging from dark violet just above the earth's curvature to the powder-blue mist of the uppermost layers, cambering against the view; the air was inert and sticky. After a time, I turned off the main drag onto a narrow backroad that appeared to lead up to a gently elevated grove. The cracked asphalt soon ceased, and in my wake, I left a track of dust which rose up around the potholes. Then the road ended, and the knoll, as minor as it had appeared, proved an illusion. The dry culms of reeds rustled several metres high, a crooked sign towering among them, designating the country border. To the left of the road was a fenced-in piece of land, grass standing tall behind the yellow paled gate, a ranch house crouching below tall acacias. The green of the trees and grasses, the tart yellow of the gate stood out against the dust and drought; it was a walled-in foreign land, a fairy-tale island set aside here at the border, uncertain employees biding their time behind closed shutters—perhaps a lure, placed by the border guards, who might have been lying burrowed in the rushes, their sights already on me. Two orioles conversed from treetop to treetop, invisible, nothing but sound.

Now only a narrow lane surrounded by tall rushes and acacias offered a view into the vastness, where behind an accumulation of darkening blues the sky met the soil.

I found my way back to the main road, crossed villages where barely anything moved, only here and there an inhabitant, standing at the cracked gate to their garden, which was surrounded by a tall fence, looking up or down the pin-straight empty street, a hand raised to their brow, although the light was no longer so bright as to compel them to shield their eyes.

Then an image turned up. I had gotten out to gaze at an undulating sea of white poppies. I had never seen white poppies before.

A gentle wind arose, causing single flower petals to tremble and come loose, sailing like feathers to the ground, revealing upon landing slender purple veins running across the white. The flower petals quickly shrank and shortly after their descent already resembled peeled skin. Yet the subject of my image was not the field of poppies, but a spot right beside it, where there ran a narrow unsurfaced road that held the remains of a puddle in the midst of all that parchedness and dustiness. An elongated strip of wet extended alongside a tyre furrow, and there, on the cast-off soil, which was just barely damp and already crusty in places, countless white butterflies had assembled, alighting and rising and hovering in the air above the residual wetness, all the while following a recondite rhythm in convened adherence to a law that could not be captured in words, but which later promised an incomprehensible yet mollifying order in the photograph, which showed nothing of the surrounding vastness or even the ribbon of horizon which had meanwhile turned nearly a uniform dark blue—a lesson to only this small strip of terrain, regarding the immortality of the butterfly.

When I reached the next town thunder was already growling, and the sky had clouded over with a dense, murky blue that was dark from dusk and storm in equal parts; only in the west did a little light hang on, brownish violet clouds drifting before it. The scent of linden filled the humid evening, a heady scent which settled on every surface as a film. It was a Saturday evening and the drunken staggered about, singing and cursing in the road, which thankfully saw hardly any traffic, while others prepared to pursue weekend pleasures, and on the central square at the yellow townhall young men revved the engines of their light blue and yellow Trabants and then got into position beside their cars, legs spread, as if to brag about having tamed those bright little creatures. Whoever didn't own a car took their beloved out for a drive on their bicycle, an artform I had never actually seen in practise until then. The girls, all done up, sat very daintily on the handlebars, elegantly holding out an arm to display a smart handbag. The cyclists and their dates rode aimless circles and figure eights in a dance of rolling lovers on a Saturday evening in a village in south-east Hungary, a performance on wheels: a man displayed himself, his sweetheart, his bicycle, the art of a cycling saunter, and later they probably went to a tavern or out dancing— maybe here they even used a word like *roadhouse*. At any rate, now was the time of exhibition, as the sinking darkness grew ever thicker and the thunder louder. Angular planes of light fell from open bar-room doors onto the dusty roadside, and when a gust of wind arose, blowing in heavy swathes of sweet linden scent, small scraps of paper danced in whirling funnels of dust. Everything was caught in this choreography of a Saturday evening in summer, and I could hardly tear myself away to search for a room.

As the sky's rumbling turned to claps of thunder and the scent of linden nestled up against a deep blackness, I sat on a folding cot in a lodging house by the small river. At least one winter's chill had burrowed into these walls and after a day in the oppressive heat, now I froze. When lightning struck nearby, the power cut out. I had opened the window to listen to the frogs, which fell silent the instant the rain swept down. I saw nothing of this night, I only lay freezing below a raw wool blanket, listening to the rain, the small river, the frogs which little by little began to croak again, yet now were calm, having dropped the fraught excitement from their sounds, and the dance of the Saturday evening couples cycling in the last light of day seemed like a dream to me. Or like a film I'd seen who-knows-where, in some other country, whose name I could no longer recollect.

On the day after the storm the sky was overcast and the air heavy with humidity. Where the roads ended the horizon hid away behind a whitish haze, the outlines of distant things indistinct in the humid air, the sounds not attributable to any particular direction, and the few people out and about now appeared to move even more slowly than the evening before. Gales and rain had ripped off most of the linden flowers, but the sweet scent still hung in the air, now even headier, teetering on the brink of wilt. I followed the course of the small river, which yesterday was only a rivulet and now, after the rain, had in fact risen over the banks here and there but was so swollen it hardly appeared capable of forward motion. The frogs croaked. In an alluvial meadow lined by poplar trees I came across pale playground equipment: a swing, a crooked seesaw, a sandbox full of dandelions and shepherd's purse. Rising up behind a row of poplar trees was a settlement of four- or five-storey apartment buildings, concrete blocks, unassailable and angular, even the balconies concrete boxes, but as if to soften the unassailability they were painted pink and yellow, the paint worn down by the dust and elements of so many summers and winters.

In the humid, misty air the village appeared to have nothing in common with the place of yesterday evening. It was a Sunday, bells clanged from several directions; I counted four church steeples. The streets remained empty, the shops and bars closed. I followed the road across the small river. It was very quiet, only the oriole called out loudly from acacia trees in the rear gardens. The acacias had advanced where people had left; they shot up tall, absorbing the groundwater that sloshed just below the surface. Most of the houses on the street appeared abandoned, their shutters hung crookedly, weeds wound around the gate posts. At the end of the road I came across the train station. An old one-storey building, painted yellow like so many of the old façades in this region, a matte, warm yellow of the past. The tracks ended here, went lost to the east in a sea of red poppies, wild sage and mullein. A turkey gobbled with its throat distended in the middle of the sea of poppies, its retinue flock warily looking on. I sat down for a moment on the bench beneath the carved wooden portico shading the train platform. A single reddish-yellow car enjoyed its Sunday break on the tracks. Beyond that was a sprawling, uncultivated field—a meadow, a no man's land—and trembling above the vastness was the air, which grew warmer and more humid, although no sun was visible. I realized I hadn't a clue where I was. Where had I washed up, what railway line terminated here? In what direction did the roads lead? Where was the nearest town whose name I knew? I followed the tracks across a narrow road that ran alongside tall storehouses clearly no longer in use. Bright plaster crumbled off the masonry walls, and the three or four levels of square openings suggested that in the past the buildings were used for dehydrating or drying something. They had been erected with an attention to and even insistence on architectonic proportions and beauty; along the upper edge ran an angular garland moulding, which embellished more than it served any particular function. Where the path intersected with a wider road, there was a railroad crossing, guarded by a small pavilion that bore the station's name, and through a window I saw a small parlour, where on a table there was an open register of train arrivals and departures. The gate was operated by a crank. In the shadowless white light of that overcast day, as I looked at the drying storehouses, northern Italy came to my mind: a scene, perhaps a film set in the Po Basin, although neither a plot nor faces occurred to me, only this light, similar buildings with crenel-like windows, and a woman who walked her bicycle down a narrow, unpeopled road. From the train station I followed the village road back towards the central square. A few cyclists, most of them women, rolled quietly past and then turned around to face me and stared, which nevertheless did not upset their equilibrium; unperturbed, they proceeded onwards, skilfully balancing on their shoulders or the handlebars of their bicycles their hoes, rakes and spades. I felt foreign under their gaze, cut free from all contexts of familiarity and belonging. A strange sensation, yet it pleased me. At every turn, this wholly unfamiliar landscape called up memories or, to a much greater extent, images, which rose from a deep repository of things set aside, things I had seen but not necessarily experienced, from films, books, old photo albums. Where in memory is the boundary between images seen and things experienced, as they say, *first hand*? The gaze is the funnel that feeds images to the conscious mind. The images become memories, are grouped anew in the memory, receive their own significances, become. I know a slightly underexposed photograph of three men, each in a different hat, posing so near to one another in front of a cherry tree that the blossoming crown encircles their faces like a garland, their faces so dark from the exposure that their expressions remain a mystery—it must have been taken somewhere around here, in one of these gardens; and how could it be said that this picture is not among my experiences when it, after all, found entrance into my childhood dreams and even the slight pucker of its surface, as well as the points of the ornamental edging, impressed themselves upon the memory of my fingertips so utterly that I believed myself capable of feeling and recognizing it blind. At every house and in every garden I thought I discerned traces that coalesced with images and voices from my memory; faces ran through my mind without my knowing their names, places I hadn't thought of for ages, and films, again and again, whose titles I could not recall, whose plots eluded me, yet which I could still place in a particular cinema, even remembering at what distance I had sat from the screen, and the smells, noises, the outline of another viewer's head in front of me, the weather outside when I left, and the closer I came to the central square, the more this town appeared to be a mysterious, unbounded prop room, a store of countless images and scenes, which here led their own lives.

By now the quiet Sunday road was once again populated by drunken, toothless men of all ages in dirty coveralls, who swayed and called out to one another unintelligible things: in other words, the bars had opened. Under the cover of sound created by the clanging Sunday bells, keys had turned the locks, opening the smoky taverns to let in the thirsty people, who after burning through the night now had to burn through the day. This strange world, which seemed to follow rules both unknown and incomprehensible, yet mysteriously familiar to me, had left me in a state of amazement that was no longer on a par with bewilderment but approached awe, and so it came as no surprise when, right before I reached the small river and the central square, I turned onto a road and found myself standing in front of a very large olive-green building, which must have been from the fifties, perhaps the early sixties, and displayed the bold lettering: *Mozi*. Cinema. What could have been more natural than a large cinema in a godforsaken town full of lost, discarded, squandered and worn-out scenes?

The glass entrance doors were equipped with refined latticework, an urban flair boasting the standard elegance of mid-twentieth-century public buildings, which appeared so out of place in this abandoned-seeming town. Who passed in and out of these doors? There were heavy curtains patterned with golden vines hanging inside in front of the locked glass doors. Through the gap between them I could make out an empty room. The wooden window and door frames were weathered, as was the edging on a display case beside the entrance. The wood exuded the smell of summer, of absorbed warmth, the dust of all the years that had pulverized the varnish. Not a healthy smell, but one loaded with spontaneous child-hood memories of holiday rentals, where the heat of summer had surfeited every last fibre and pore of things. Hanging in the display case were a few bluish photos, which inspired vague associations, and a sheet of paper, slipped down, with a list of dates and times. Not until I had noticed and decoded the lettering that flaunted large on the façade, which, just like the door's latticework, was designed according to ideas of a bygone era, did I identify the faded photo-graphs in the display case. They were scenes from the film *Megáll az idő. Time Stands Still.* Five out of ten Hungarians undoubtedly still counted it among their favourite movies. It matched the lettering on the olive-green façade, although the film itself is only simulating, offering a painstaking look back at the time when letterings like this were designed. I crossed back to the other side of the street and examined the building thoroughly. It appeared enormous for the small town. A splendid cinema in a no-man's-land of possibilities.

I wandered every which way through town, returning to the

outlying train station, then back down the linden street without lindens, and I determined that the cinema building extended to the corner of the main intersection in town, where it met the post office at a right angle. Mail, cinema, police. The pillars of order. Treetops towered over the locked entrance gate that joined the cinema and the police station.

Meanwhile, an oppressive stillness characteristic of Sunday afternoons had descended, and I unpacked my camera and tripod and set up across from the cinema. No one was out and about any more, the drinkers had all once again drunk themselves silent, and everyone else was chewing their gristly Sunday meat, its smell wafting from the houses. I didn't want to create a stir; I didn't want anyone to ask me questions that I could not answer. But it didn't matter how long I struggled, looking through the viewfinder—I found no frame for the view, no gaze, no solution for a picture capable of facing a future beholder.

I set out on my return trip and observed that the poppies had dropped their petals in the storm and now stretched their greenish, subtly crowned little pates; there was nothing but these heads, seas, multitudes of heads in the milky light and this lull, anticipating hot days that would dry the seeds inside them until every gust of wind filled the air with a quiet rattling. Everything around—the indistinct vastness, the matte tones, the strange nylon tunnels of the melon farms—all stepped into relation with the place that I had become acquainted with, the straight roads, the many empty houses, the small train station and the cinema.

The next day I walked around Budapest in a daze, saw *Moscow*

Does Not Believe in Tears as part of Russian Week at a cinema in District V that I rarely visited, although it reminded me greatly of my youth. No one in the cinema seemed to be watching the film for the first time: they sighed and laughed in expectation of familiar scenes and were satisfied when all proceeded as expected, as remembered, as ever. One piece of reliable history from the last century.

The Hungarian word for cinema is *mozi*, short for *mozgókép*: moving images. An enticingly foreign word. At the start of this century, Budapest, too, was still a cinema city and when I moved there from London, in the dust of summer, in the vicinity of my downtown apartment there must have been half-a-dozen *mozik*, arthouses backed by tradition and a regular viewing public. Hungarian films had led me to this Central European city in the first place, where the cinemas operated so differently than they did in London. Even if I had moved districts often, I had still lived, without interruption, in London for longer than anywhere else in my life, and accordingly I had also gone to the cinema there much more often than in any other city. London was not a cinema city in the way that Paris, Budapest, Vienna and Berlin were, but due to its sheer size it had many theatres, of which quite a few no longer exist today or have changed to the point of unrecognition, remodelled according to notions that grant seeing and the space for seeing only an ancillary role, overshadowed by ostensible amenities meant to justify the price of admission, transforming a trip to the cinema into a luxury good, and thus declaring it dispensable. Of all the cinemas I visited there, only one has remained relatively the same, right down to the slightly musty smell that envelops me as soon as the door shuts out the restless street, where so much is decided—in suffering and conflict and waning hopes. I remember very well the many entrance doors, lobbies and auditoriums between the East Finchley Phoenix, the Rio in Dalston and the Ritzy in Brixton, being the outermost points on my map of screens. One of my favourite cinemas was the old Everyman in Hampstead, located at the time in a small, ascending alley; the seats were uncomfortable. *Everyman, I will go with thee and be thy guide* might inevitably pop into some people's minds when they hear the name: lines from an anonymous mystery play. The cinema as a support, a companion for everyman, a guiding star and an escort, a refuge for all, a place that offered shelter to innumerable solitudes, hopes and dreams, a shelter with a view. Today there is an Everyman chain that operates under the illusion that it is possible to replicate a small, one-of-a-kind reel cinema where you can hole up inside Ozu's *Tokyo Story* on a dreary Christmas Eve, yet the replicas recall nothing of the original Everyman of Hampstead in the late twentieth century.

Even more than the cinemas themselves, I remember the trips home after the film, on foot, an hour or more, when after the ride there and a cinema ticket there wasn't enough money left for the bus ride home; I remember these trips in the wind of the Thames smelling of the sea; in a thin autumn rain; on soft, electric summer nights with illuminated busses whirring past, and howling police cars and ambulances, walking by masses of people in front of the closing bars and through very silent residential streets where the shadows of cats flitted across, and hungry foxes walked zigzag from dustbin to dustbin, searching for one whose lid was easily nudged. From Everyman, however, the walk was downhill, and the view was vast; the streetlights spread out, and a string of lights from the elevated North London Line extended in regular intervals across the night sky above. From the farther lying cinemas I would have occasionally preferred to take the bus home, when caught in a drizzle or the winter wind, but these long trips, the sequences of images, the sounds, the tatters of sentences in the tremendous open air of the city were all part of the cinema experience, forming spaces between the framed vision and the boundless arbitrariness of the visible world all around: transitional zones where what I had seen in the cinema settled and began to take effect, wreathed by passing impressions, which grew paler with time, but never waned entirely. The footpath over the old Hungerford Bridge swayed, echoed, trembled disconcertingly beneath our feet, while the trains pulled into Charing Cross, groaning and shrieking and near enough to touch, or else they left the station, rattling the yellow signs with appeals to witnesses of recent 'incidents' to come forward. At every step you were met by your own memories, loitering at every street joining: of earlier walks from the cinema back to the city, to the north, the way home, and all of it was woven together to form a separate layer of life.

And now I was in Pest, wreathed by cinemas, all of them lying on or near the ring road, which girded the centre of town and shot off the major arterial roads that led into the plains east of the city. My habits quickly changed in this much slower city. The air was heavy from the dust of the façades decaying below bird droppings and stove smoke. When an old apartment building was razed or simply up and collapsed under some imperceptible deathblow—a concise, deliberate pound of the fist was all it took, they said—then curtains of dust would hang in the alleys, clouding the view. In addition to the life of the alleys and the streets there was the life of the courtyards. It took place in the open corridors from which you entered the apartments and which enclosed the yard. These galleries were stages, each one for itself, where the inhabitants rehearsed their roles in life, performing them over and over again. There was the theatre of pickled cukes swaying in large jars full of a cloudy fermenting liquid; it was fraught with occasional irritable exchanges about the state of the cukes and a few times even reached a tragic climax when a saucer became suctioned onto the jar such that the fermentation gas had no way to escape and the pressure caused the glass to burst.

At dusk the courtyard theatre closed, the televisions switched on in the apartments, small bats whirred between geraniums and pickle jars, the empty space of the courtyard filled with the mute, flickering reflection of the screens, and I set out for the cinema.

Occasionally late at night when I returned to my apartment I would see a certain neighbour lingering at the gallery railing, smoking. Julika was old, difficult to say how old, but presumably over eighty. She wore sleeveless smocks washed pale, their weak floral patterns still vaguely perceptible, and she was the cuke queen of her floor, her wards all faultless like gently puffed-up new moons buoying in the increasingly murky liquid. Yet above all else, Julika was a chain smoker. Late at night she would stand, a silent shadow, positioned between her apartment door and the gallery railing, the muffled sound of a television programme leaking from the interior of her apartment, the burning tip of her cigarette moving in the dark. Occasionally she flailed her arms, perhaps to scare off the bats, and in that moment, cloaked in her shadow, it appeared as if she had wings. Sometimes she would quietly call down to me goodnight as I opened the door to my apartment. One evening she asked where

I had been, and I said: At the cinema. Oh, the cinema! she said, her voice raw from cigarette smoke, Once I had a fellow who was a great cinema man. That ended the conversation for her; she stubbed her cigarette in the plant pot beside the door and went into her apartment, leaving me to wonder what a 'great cinema man' was.

In summer there were regular hairstyling afternoons on the gallery. A hairdresser named Ildikó came with a little suitcase full of styling tools and did my neighbours' hair. Weather allowing, they sat outside in their slips at folding tables, and ate cake and had Ildikó crimp and dye their hair in a cloud of ceaseless pattering, while Julika, in curlers, stood on the balcony, leaned against the railing, and smoked one cigarette after the other. Behind thick glasses, her eyes twinkled below drooping lids, and something about her gaze was piercing. If my neighbours had something to tell me, they sent Ildikó, since she spoke German, and they evidently deemed that more appropriate than Hungarian for important matters. Ildikó informed me when the electricity and gas meters would be read, that the interior door to the stairwell was to be double-locked at all times, day and night, and that my flowers on the gallery had aphids. In addition, Ildikó told me that between her hairstyling appointments with my neighbours she worked on a Danube cruise ship which travelled between Vienna and the Danube Delta, and it was on board that she had learned German. Ildikó laughed frequently and for no apparent reason, and she enjoyed talking. Before her life as a hairstylist she worked at a tile factory in the western part of the country, but it was too loud for her there. It was a place with a difficult name, she said, Székesfehérvár. Repeat after me, she said: Szé-kes-fe-hér-vár. I'm not sure if she was satisfied with my pronunciation; she left it at this short lesson. I heard the women outside talking and laughing, often about money, about buying things and not having things and about men. Tell us again, what was it like with your Laci? The women called over, after Julika's curlers had been removed and Ildikó ran a comb through her thin grey hair, trying to give a form to the limp waves. Was Laci the one whom Julika had described to me as a 'great cinema man'? Oh, my Laci, Julika said, my Laci—he was a son of a gun. From snippets of the conversation that followed I deduced that Laci really had run a cinema, and at the height of his commercial success Julika had sold tickets for him at the window and afterwards torn them when it was time to let viewers into the auditorium—she had even owned a flashlight—while Laci, in her words, operated the machines.

One day Ildikó invited me on her ship, which was anchored in Budapest. It was an extremely hot day when I climbed aboard, the city lay in a haze, shimmering and shadowless, as it often does before stormy evenings. On the ship I saw neither a captain nor a crew, nor wavy-haired passengers. It was gapingly empty. Ildikó ran a tiny salon on board, which I was allowed to visit after she showed me the communal rooms, a luxury cabin and the small kiosk at the reception, which she also ran on the side. Although she was not the ship's owner, she appeared enormously proud that day, describing herself, using one of her favourite expressions, as a *full-blooded businesswoman*, for whom hairstyling was just the beginning. She brought me up to the deck, from which point Budapest, under a characteristic whitish-grey summer sky, looked oddly different than it did from either bank of the Danube or from one of the bridges. I had never been on a ship larger than one of the small joyride steamers on the Rhine, and as I stood there at the railing I had to think about the film *The Danube Exodus*, about the ship as a migratory pod, about how the splinters of film flowed and about the eeriness of the 'real' faces from the home-movie footage. At last Ildikó introduced me to her fiancé, who worked on the ship as a waiter and was in the middle of folding napkins into neat cardinal's hats for future occasions. His name was Ilija and he was Bulgarian. He was tall and had black curls and a bright smile that never faded from his face. He served me a coffee and raved about life as a ship waiter. His favourite city was Bratislava, his least favourite was Belgrade. He himself was from a city called Ruse on the Danube and he found it extraordinary that a single river managed to flow through so many capitals. He loved his homeland but preferred to talk about Uzbekistan, where his father had relocated because of the better pay for bus drivers, and where in summer it was so hot that the bus occasionally became stuck in the asphalt, while he, the bus driver's son, a teenager with a future in the cruise industry, watched adventure movies in an open-air Uzbek cinema, looking up every once in a while, and incidentally glimpsing the stars. Welcome in Bulgaria, he said in farewell from the deck, and as I walked down the gangway to exit the boat he assumed the role of captain, placing a hand on his black curls in salute.

After a time I drove back to the south-east. I was gripped by the cinema façade, the poppy fields, the white butterflies, the roads all leading to the horizon, the slowness, the train station. It was a weekday and below a blue sky the last bit of linden scent had also tipped into wither, the hollyhocks teemed with firebugs, and an arid rattle filled the poppy fields in anticipation of the harvest, when the seed heads would burst open and the grey seeds, freed of all chaff by a centrifugal sieve, would chatter in the collecting bins. There was no vacancy at the lodging house, as all the beds were occupied by adults supervising a group of Romanian children. The children had come from mountain villages, where Hungarian was the spoken language, to this place, a few kilometres past the border, in the plains, in their country of linguistic belonging, where they slept in bunkhouses and ate at long tables, crowded in small, non-native groups around the candy at CBA supermarket and spent their afternoons at the swimming pool. For ten days they remained in their assigned homeland, and after that they were brought back to the place where they were from, and new children arrived from the mountains of Romania. I was told that I might find a place to stay in the next town over, on the other side of the railroad tracks. I drove through the exhausted midday landscape. Acacia groves, cornfields, sunflower fields. A small apple orchard. The sunlight reflected off the leaves of the trees, oddly lustrous. The street crossed the tracks twice. Once I saw in the distance a small train, red-yellow, like the one I had seen at the abandoned station on my first stay there. Like a toy conducted by an invisible hand, it moved through the fields and groves already pale from the heat, a foreign body. In the neighbouring town I found a bed in a dormitory recently vacated by Romanian children. I had it all to myself. That evening I sat by the window, staring out at the street bounded by lindens, watching couples dance to Hungarian pop music in the flickering light of a streetlamp on the pavement in front of a bar. One of the dancers left his partner from time to time, retreating to his bicycle where he bit into a salami he kept tucked away in his pannier. The dance carried on until after midnight, cicadas chirring in the pauses between songs. I sat by the window until the tired barkeep chased off the dancers. The large, empty dormitory stretched behind me, a dark cavern with no remaining trace of the children sent to Hungary. The sheets on the bed were threadbare, no doubt from being sent through the mangle at a commercial laundry countless times already. The blankets folded at the foot of the beds were so thin that a chill coursed through my blood when I imagined having to rely on one some cool night. As the dancers slowly departed, their laughter, song and bellows were audible from an increasing distance, and the barkeep ran a broom across the pavement, as if to sweep away traces of the dance. Then he locked up, and aside from cicadas all was silent. The night arched high and ample over the flat land. Every village was a different film, as it appeared to me. Every window a cinema.

The next morning I walked through the *mozi* village, drawing curious eyes. It was a weekday and everyone was pursuing their slow tasks: sweeping, inspecting the cherry trees on the grass verges between the houses and roadways, collecting fallen fruit, cycling with encumbrances, loitering, looking, pattering. The street grid left no possibility for getting lost, and I always returned to the crossing with the post office, the cinema and the police station. In the trees along the languid small river orioles called. Dogs roamed the wayside, cats slinked past the masonry walls and rested, motionless in the grass, waiting for prey. Out back behind the butcher were stacked boxes of poultry parts, swarming with flies. The butcher, wearing a long apron, entered the yard, shooed away the flies, picked up a box and carried it in. Aside from the CBA supermarket, the town had a Chinese restaurant and an ice cream parlour, as well as a greengrocer and a fruit shop located in a semi-basement at whose entrance a barefoot woman now stood, a hand raised to her brow as she looked up and down the pavement. It was set deeper than the road, which extended like a dam between lindens and chestnut trees. A bicycle shop opened its doors and a tall man carried colourful children's and women's bicycles out onto the pavement, to attract customers. He walked leisurely, his head pulled in slightly between his hunched shoulders, a bike in each hand, like a muscleman at a funfair. On a side street I noticed an inscription on the front wall of an elongated shed and thought I recognized the word *mozi* in the pale, crumbling block letters. I heard the strung-out, plaintive whistle of a train getting into gear, which then proceeded to cross the street between the lowered gates on its way to the town where I had slept. I must have passed by the *mozi* half a dozen times before someone approached and asked if I was looking for something. I would like to view the cinema, I said. Do you want to buy the cinema? the man asked. He was short and had black hair, and in his eyes a sudden fervour twinkled. He put on a friendly face. Yes, perhaps I want to buy the cinema, I replied.

Inside the bicycle shop he introduced me to the tall, slightly stooped man named József, whom I had observed earlier unlocking the door and carrying out his wares. Without a bicycle you were nothing in this region. In the dim rear of the shop, in addition to Csepel bicycles and bike tubes, I saw sewing machines and used computers. They bore little name cards, some with numbers, perhaps representing the repair cost or the amount they had been pawned for. József would show me the cinema after lunch. A short time later I recognized him among the many cyclists riding to the edge of town, lunchboxes balanced on their handlebars. They all went to fill their plates at the canteen kitchen, a custom that nearly moved me in its collective simplicity and fidelity to a time when everyone went to the factory to work, when everyone was kept in supply. A custom in tune with my old foreign-language textbooks. On my rounds that morning I had seen the women stepping out of the kitchen facilities, sweating, approaching the townhall, where they would smoke, pull off their headscarves and shake out their hair, almost invariably dyed a copper red. Through the open windows I could see other women standing by large aluminium kettles. The radio played pop music that reminded me of the previous evening and the dancers under the trees in the streetlight.

Around lunchtime the cinema façade was in the blazing sun, with not a single strip of shadow offering protection, and I meandered short routes, going wherever I found cover from the sun, all the while counting, in the dead midday streets, thirty bars and bottle shops—or at least that's how I translated *italbolt*, a word with no connection to Italy, in this language which had hitherto denied everything familiar to me. I already saw József approaching in the distance. Now it was obvious he had built his bicycle himself: the handlebars were very high, making it so that the saddle, which as it happens was equipped with a little backrest, allowed the cyclist to lean back slightly, his arms stretched upwards. Later that day it occurred to me that the bicycle and József's posture reminded me of motorcycles from the film *Easy Rider*. He must have seen it when he was young. Perhaps the images and scenes had filled him with a perpetual longing for a taste of the mad life that then found its expression in this self-built bicycle and, in his vision, lent a degree of adventurousness to cycling in that boundless-seeming plain, where every path inevitably led to the horizon.

As if sprouted from the ground, the small, black-haired middle-man suddenly stood in front of the cinema as well, nodding at me and smiling as József poked a key in the slumbering lock. Opening the door required a bit of force; it rasped loudly against the stone floor. A cool, damp smell wafted from the interior when József parted the heavy curtains of imitation brocade, a slightly musty testimony to a belief in splendid things, as every cinema is due; a belief in the ritual of passing from the street into the cinema, reaching first the foyer, with a ticket counter and a *büfé*, the small concession stand, and the coat check, before entering the auditorium. The foyer was very large. A dull, pastelly brown colour with a hint of purple prevailed there on the doors, the skirting boards and the windowsills, while angular pillars supported the ceiling and gave the room a touch of something ceremonious, as in a great hall. On the walls hung photographs of once-famous actors, while a large concrete square on the floor not covered by linoleum revealed something of the past: back before they had mounted, somewhat crookedly, the convector radiators to the walls below the windows, the building was heated by a stove, perhaps a tall, tiled stove, tended to by the cashier or the usher. The windows looked out onto an overgrown backyard, and the windowsills over the crooked radiators were littered with dead flies. In the empty, dirty entrance room I imagined eager viewers crowding in, the air full of the smell of their jackets wet from rain, how they stood in line, waiting to check their jackets and coats. There must have been at least two employees, one to sell tickets and one to operate the coat check, and someone also had to work the *büfé*, tiny as it was. The doors from the foyer to the auditorium were open. Light also poured into the darkness of the auditorium from the doors on the opposite side, but these two streams of light never met: it was dark at the centre of the mustard-yellow seating rows. The opposite door led to the exit corridor, where a wall was decorated with photographs of actors. You entered the auditorium through the foyer and exited by the opposite corridor, which, due to the hopper windows installed just beneath the ceiling, had the air of a provisional workshop; the large door leading out to the street was unadorned and aside from the portraits, now covered in dust and hung much too high for a passing look, there was nothing there to distract the viewer as they walked out of the cinema's interior, the many snatches of images still floating in their minds, and into the entirely different world outside, so foreign after a film, where it might rain or be bitterly cold, with no connection whatsoever to the weather on screen. Reality catches up with you, it is said, when, after enjoying a vast prairie aglow in sunlight in a Western the viewers are released outside, where cold sleet falls on their faces—but occasionally the question arises: What is reality? Most notably, however, we can conclude from the entrance and exit doors that a new crowd of film enthusiasts had already gathered in the foyer by the time a programme came to an end.

A very beautiful cinema, commented the small black-haired man at my side. Over three hundred seats. He looked at me, hopeful.

Józsi had climbed a staircase at the end of the foyer. Once my eyes had adjusted to the darkness of the auditorium I noticed him far overhead, above the balcony, where he stood behind a dimly lit glass panel and waved.

He had gone straight to the projection booth, where two silvergrey projectors gazed idly onto the seat rows and the large, bare main wall. There was no screen covering the plaster. The windows to the garden were encrusted with fly droppings, and the black crumbs of their desiccated corpses covered the windowsills and the floor below. Lying around the projector were film reels. Józsi stood ankle-deep in coiled celluloid, holding a strip up to the murky light of the window encrusted in fly droppings. I still remember that, he said. It was a romance. Or something along those lines.

Józsi had been the cinema's projectionist. For over twenty years he screened films here, having learned from the former projectionist, first working as his assistant, and later taking over his position. Six days a week, sometimes twice a day; Wednesdays the cinema was closed. On Tuesdays we had an 'international film club', and we showed everything, Józsi said. Sergio Leone and Kurosawa and Truffaut and Fassbinder, and many others from neighbouring countries. Yugoslavia, Czechoslovakia, Poland; sometimes even the directors came. One director from Yugoslavia brought along a suckling pig and we roasted it out back in the yard, Józsi said. After the cinema shut its doors, Józsi put on a new hat and began repairing bicycles, sewing machines and computers.

I held up the strip that Józsi had carefully laid back down on the ground. After studying it a bit in the dim light I recognized the final scene from *The Hairdresser's Husband*. I remembered the last film I had seen featuring the same actor. Called *Wind with the Gone*, back then it had a short run in a small cinema on the upper end of Burggasse in Vienna. A film about reels of film. That seemed to me a nearly ridiculous coincidence. The short, black-haired man stood at the door and grinned, somewhat agonized; perhaps his agony was on account of the dirt, the flies, the pale green wash of the walls, puckered and peeling. Or had he arranged everything just as it was, and now was insecure about the coherence of his work? Had he written a screenplay involving the unravelled film reels, in reference to the Argentinian film featuring the actor from *The Hairdresser's Husband*? Were Józsi's comments also his invention? Who was playing whom? He squinted, as if to better see something up close, but he didn't move. Three-hundred-and-fifty-six seats, Józsi said. Three-hundred-and-fifty-six after the final renovation. And a full house was not all that unusual.

Every cinema has its own specific atmosphere and energy. It cannot really be defined and certainly cannot be pinned down to anything concrete. Wherever there are projectors, a cinema will develop its own inimitable expression, composed of a blend of the projector's glow, expectations, dreams and dust, as well as a variety of interplays in proportions found only there: between outside and inside; stories and history; the solitude of each individual gaze looking out from the dark and the world that opens up and assimilates all the gazes. Every cinema has its regulars and random guests, its nappers and whisperers and its smell of dust, linoleum, the street, sweat and perfume, its own darkness, brightened somewhat by the illuminated signs directing to the toilets and emergency exits. The cinema is a space of expectations that are seldom let down—not even by a bad film, since every time, no matter what, you end up seeing further than you had before, exploring a horizon that would not exist without the screen.

Located in the middle of a Hungarian village which had once been a big town, this cinema, too, had its singularity; it filled the air over the mustard-yellow retractable seats and slowly awoke in response to the gazes it sought. Everything here had been sleeping for a long time: the seats, the thick drapes on the doors between the foyer and the auditorium, the strips of celluloid and the projectors. The thin lines of communication that were once spun between the gaze and the screen had also been sleeping and were now caught on something or tangled between the seat legs, left to their own devices. From up there, looking through the pane that separated the projection booth from the uppermost rows of balcony seats, I could picture what the cinema had once meant to people here; a piece of life, a space of refuge and a horizon of hope had existed between these walls, in this town where the horizon was, after all, everywhere, at the end of every street. The people I had observed outside, the slow-motion cyclers and pavement sweepers, the field labourers and gardeners pulling up withered plants in community plots—I couldn't really picture them sitting on these retractable seats; despite all their curious stares, they seemed so withdrawn, as if they had gotten out of the habit of looking into a vastness—yet they must have been the ones who filled the foyer and the auditorium, who checked their coats and jackets for a screening of *The Hairdresser's Husband*, for instance, and who gleaned from that film something that could never be fully wiped away. The mere presence of the celluloid strips on the floor of the projector booth was enough to guarantee it, regardless of how dirty and scratched they might have been.

The short black-haired man told me his name as we left the cinema. He was Zoran, he was Serbian, and he offered services of all kinds. This is a Serbian area, a Serbian town, even, he said in passing, as if to justify his Serbian identity in this particular location. He pointed to one of the church steeples in the street and told me it was the Serbian church, beside which was the Serbian school. Multi-ethnic Hungary could be found around every corner and at every border; the strictly guarded crossings seemed an arbitrary intervention in this open country leading to the horizon. I suddenly suspected that

Zoran awaited payment for his services as a self-proclaimed town guide. No, no, don't mention it, he said when I reached for my wallet. He left once he realized I wasn't going anywhere, and I wondered if he was hanging around some gateway, crouching and observing me as I scrutinized the building from outside. It appeared larger to me, now that I had seen its interior; it had a presence that cast everything else in shadow. Olive green and a darker tone, the washed brown-violet of the interior paint job, a colour that recalled dried blood outside, on the large surface of the façade. The most beautiful thing about it was the typeface, its angular daring, which bespoke a certain tempo, a desire for speed that retained a trace of Buster Keaton's dynamic chaotization of the world, yet which preferred to be constructive, almost reasonable: a typeface characteristic of a retired, yet not forgotten, vision of the future that would have suited the drawings in my Polish textbooks; the pointed tails of the letters referenced a time when everyone went to the cinema every day, rushed there, in fact, as a matter of course, frequenting the screen in order to train their gaze, to fill the gap between the eye and the projection surface with their own associations and the pictorial threads which they would then spin further. Perhaps this past, which had slipped into the realm of the fabulous, was what weighed on people's minds here every day, slowing their every movement. The absence of any promise whatsoever, combined with the great void of a landscape defined only by what it lacked.

Indeed, it was a land of dearth, a region of voids. If you stood at the edge of the village, the sky accounted for four-fifths of the field of vision. Sunflowers, corn and acacias defined the rest. Here and there a collapsed farmstead, an abandoned vehicle or equipment in a field. Even without being exposed to some external trauma the mudbrick houses in this region subside after only a few years of vacancy: the groundwater sloshes just below the soil, and the rising dampness softens the walls. The village had once been a big town, but in the last ten or twelve years two-thirds of its occupants had either moved away, died or disappeared. There was a lack of work, of money, of prospects. Mawkish evocations of a homeland had fused with bitter dissatisfaction over the poverty, spoiling the mood for whoever remained. At the same time, life *had* once been good. The place had once been bustling, with a hotel, a prison, small businesses, a bar with gypsy music. And a cinema. Everyone had something to say about the cinema. Which films they saw there, how often they went, their preferred seats, the cost of admission. Saturday evenings young couples went, and on Sundays the children were sent for a matinee, an animation or a fairy-tale film. The cinema opened its doors in the sixties, under the name '*Alkotmány Mozi*': a cinema in honour of the constitution. It was not the first cinema in town, they said; before this one there was a cinema housed in a renovated work shed, run by a film enthusiast. From the seats down to the projectors, this film enthusiast had acquired everything on his own and was married to his cinema, so to speak, or at least that's what people said, but because the wooden benches were always crowded with viewers, one day he applied to city council with a proposal to build a splendid cinema. What town deserved a 'cinema of the constitution' if not this one, a town which itself was even the subject of a film, played and propagandized again and again, into the seventies: *Felsz-abadulás*, a film about the Soviet Army's liberation of this small town, the first town on Hungarian soil to be liberated in September

44

1944. The summer I discovered the cinema, as I got down to cleaning the interior, washing windows, laundering curtains and lathering the seats with lavender soap, I heard about this film every day, as if it were chief witness to the cinema's former greatness and guarantor of its future revival. Each morning a certain employee from the municipal administration stopped by on his rattling bicycle, offering suggestions for a future programme. Each day he came up with new *mozi* reminiscences, about films he had seen there, talks that were held there, the long lines at the ticket counter for certain films. He often ended by referencing the singularity and significance of the liberation film, which he absolutely wanted to experience in this cinema again.

The projectionist Józsi, on the other hand, spoke with fondness about the first cinema, run by Deutsch László, the film enthusiast who had paved the way for the large cinema. Józsi had seen and even been allowed to thread his first films there, under László's attentive gaze. To this day, my fingers haven't forgotten it, he said with pride, holding up a large hand to show me, every groove black from lubricating oil, his fingertips covered in calluses, but Józsi insisted that his first encounter with that smooth, soft and yet obstinately fragile celluloid material still dwelt inside his fingers, it had never let him go. In a long, arduous process he had taken over the projectionist position from Deutsch László, who until the end of his life, which coincided with the so-called regime change, had visited the cinema daily and performed small hand movements, following the films only from the window of the projection booth, even though it meant squeezing into the corner on a stool beside the projectors, while Józsi, in his words, operated the machines. When I followed Józsi's directions to the original cinema, I found myself once again in front

45

of the abandoned house, where I thought I had deciphered the word *mozi* on an adjacent building resembling a work shed. As if a shadow, the letters appeared on the crumbling plaster of the front wall, yet this time I couldn't make them out; they were mere parts of letters that could have been transformed into any word, simply by adding a line or two, dots, a stroke here or there. In places the gate to the yard was so eaten away by rust that you could peer through it, into the wild garden, and from a certain angle I caught sight of a jar, set down on the sill of a half-broken window beside the entrance, and it reminded me of the pickle containers on the gallery in Budapest. In the grey liquid were small, dark shadows, yet unlike the dreamily floating cucumber sickles of Budapest, these ones didn't move at all.

Back on the gallery in front of my apartment in Budapest my neighbours asked about my trip with curiosity and even suspicion, as if there was something not quite right about my repeated trips to the bleak south-east. The hairstylist Ildikó spoke disparagingly about the Alföld. What's there to see there, anyway, she said. Cinema, I replied, and she laughed, embarrassed—perhaps she thought it was a joke. I said a few words about the large cinema which had been closed for a few years, in the half-abandoned town. My neighbours looked at me uncomprehending. No one goes to the cinema any more, the hairstylist explained. If people see you at the cinema, they think you don't have enough money for a TV. Or a VCR. It's that simple. That's why no one wants to go. The other women nodded and murmured something, and clever Gaby, who was studying accounting and occasionally came to clean the apartment of her father, the building's caretaker, said: Anyone can do the maths.

At dusk Julika shuffled over to me and placed a well-worn envelope of photographs on my table. That was my cinema man, she explained. They were old pictures, smooth and glossy, with beautiful, slightly yellowed scalloped edges. One of them showed a young Julika, her dark hair in a pageboy cut, wearing glasses already then; smiling, she poses beside a walrus-moustached man in a pinstripe suit who proudly holds a film reel in front of his stomach. There were perhaps a dozen images and he was in all of them: in work clothes in front of a work bench; beside Julika in front of a film poster, on which I could make out a carousel; with other men in suits. The cinema was his life, she said in a voice that sounded so artificial, as if she had read that empty phrase from a tattered piece of paper just fished out of her apron pocket. From down south, where they stand on pumpkins in order to see all the way to who-knows-where, that's where he was from. They need cinemas there. Julika took her photographs and bade me good night. She smoked another cigarette, while the television images flickered behind her windows, in no need of a viewer. Later I saw the outline of her head, black against the screen.

On Saturdays I liked to go to the flea market held on the unused terrain behind Keleti Station, by the sidetrack overgrown with weeds, where disused shunters and freight wagons stood. It was a large market, which opened on Saturday at dawn. Here you found above all the poor, selling things to other poor people: unnecessary things, lifted things, occasionally items gained with a guilty conscience, for instance plundered from the apartment of a recently deceased neighbour, before anyone authorized had entered, to say nothing of an heir. They proffered bedsheets full of holes that smelled of soap suds, leaking gas pipes and sewage, unearthed from downtrodden apartments in old rental buildings, and perhaps worth a meagre penny. The vendors were clueless, however, about the worth of their eggshell-thin pre-war porcelain and the photographs, which they handed over for just a few hundred forints, being as they were much likelier to believe in the value of stainless steel moka-pot field sets issued for military service, or souvenirs from Vienna—the Ferris wheel in a snow flurry, for instance—or misshapen orange 'Western lamps' from the seventies. I had a favourite stand. It was run by an elderly, portly man named Feri and his two slow-witted daughters. Feri was a shrewd merchant who, with inscrutable pre-sentiments, always pulled something out of his sleeve that awoke in me overwhelming memories or a curious sense of astonishment. When I first found Feri's stand he spoke in a broken falsetto; then for a while he was absent and whenever I asked after him his daughters only said, No idea, and looked past me. After being gone a few weeks, he returned with an artificial voice box, which his colleagues and customers marvelled at reverentially. Say something, Feri, they begged him. What should I say, Feri asked, and that was already enough—it didn't matter where he was standing, his artificial voice chirred from some utterly unexpected spot, as if he were standing behind the person he stood in front of, and their delight at this effect knew no bounds. One Saturday, among the goods exhibited at Feri's stand I found an object that awoke my curiosity, although I didn't know where to begin with it. It was an elongated, rectangular, thin piece of scratched metal, appointed with a guillotine cutter and several clips, below which it would have been possible to insert or push a flat strip of material across a transparent glass surface. Chirring, Feri explained that this instrument was used, for example in projection booths, to repair torn film strips. I turned the device

48

every which way, considering it from all sides, and tried to imagine what it might be like to repair celluloid in great haste. I had never thought about the effort that went into repairing torn film, but standing there, examining that object, I was able to imagine the precision and the speed, the dexterity and the composure it required, while the audience chomped at the bit in the auditorium. I paid for the object and carried it back to my apartment, without taking another look around the flea market.

A few years before I discovered the cinema in that south-eastern Hungarian town, I saw two films about tangled film strips and cinemas in remote locations. Around the time that *Wind with the Gone* came out, set in Argentina, the film *One Winter Behind God's Back* was released in Hungary. The phrase 'behind God's back' is a Hungarian idiom referring to a very remote place, but it might hold an intimation of ethical questionability for those unfamiliar with it. Although the plots and characters in the two films are entirely dissimilar, both are concerned with the cinema as a place of refuge and hope, and with film as material—exposed, developed and in disarray. At the time, the materiality of film was already beginning to lose significance in real life, and by the end of the century—the cinema century—the cinema's importance as an elaborately equipped destination for film was also put to question. In both films, the cinema as a place is romanticized in a fabulous way that involves geographical remoteness and inaccessibility, and a state of uncertainty pertaining to its belonging in the world and reality. Even by the mid-nineties, aside from a few extravagant resurrections of pastoral cinema idylls found in attractive coastal towns in England, for instance, only metropolitan cinemas had a chance at holding their own: places where a visit to the cinema was not a decision born of necessity but where every ticket purchased could be regarded as an individual rejection of other forms of visual mediation. In both films the respective fictive cinema's significance is contingent on its remoteness, its extreme marginality, its hopeless location 'behind God's back', giving people the chance to look into a vastness, in a place from which everything else is turned away. There is no other option, so no one can dismiss cinemagoers as being too poor for other forms of visual entertainment. In both films, the unconventional handling of the damaged celluloid material, which has been robbed of its context along with its tense, is more the result of cluelessness (What now? What to see?) than it is an inventive examination of the possibilities that open up when the material is estranged from its purpose (How to look?). Nevertheless, in this form the strips of celluloid unfurl an entirely distinct, unrepeatable magic which is theirs alone; they are beauties from a different time, dreamily waving goodbye, revealing themselves as a material that yields to a foreign fable and nourishes a self-perpetuating longing.

I kept thinking about the film strips I came across in the old cinema, and months after discovering the town, when I began to clean the place up, I didn't throw them away. They were testimony. Perhaps they would have made for good secondary material in a found-footage film, but that found footage didn't exist. Later Józsi used them as test material, once the projectors were up and running and the main wall had been plastered smooth and painted a flawless white, holding its own as a projection surface, in place of the decomposing canvas screen.

Yet even after that, the strips remained neatly rolled up in the projection booth. They were testimony to something I couldn't quite pin down, and I was apprehensive to throw them away. They belonged to a past I had no access to, and I thought they might still contain and perhaps divulge something to help me understand the place. The place itself, the idiosyncratic progression of time there, the emptiness and the vastness which unremittingly invited one to look, in order to learn from the *how*. I was every bit as reluctant to throw away these worn-out film strips as I was to throw away old negatives, even of shots I deemed entirely useless, which I would never even print, but which nevertheless retained the mysterious possibility of perhaps containing something that might one day become apparent and divulge itself, after I had already spent so much time searching for it. Little by little I cleaned the boxes, made from thin wood with securable compartments for the individual film reels. The compartments were opened and closed by a vertical latch and numbered one to twelve, from left to right. Eventually I stowed away the celluloid strips there. The simplicity of these boxes, suitable only for this very purpose, was moving and beautiful, but the boxes were not salvageable for any lasting use, since the dampness of the building had attacked the back covers made from thin plywood, and even gnawed at the legs, which tapered towards the ground. They wouldn't be able to hold the heavy film rolls for long. The celluloid strips, discharged of any function, would coalesce with the decaying wood, forming a helpless unit.

The next time I visited, I brought Józsi the gadget from the Budapest flea market. He stopped working on a large, heavy women's bicycle and procured from below the counter a very similar object. It was larger and heavier, the metal frame more scratched, and it was dented in one corner. But it functioned in the same way as my found object. Józsi returned to mending the bicycle; sitting on a chair in the dusky rear of the shop was an elderly woman who obviously was in urgent need of her bicycle. Olga used to work in the cinema, Józsi explained. Olga nodded. She wore a white blouse, a black pleated skirt and heavy black shoes that laced up above her ankles. Her entire outfit looked like an overhauled uniform from days past, from a workplace that might have been transported, overnight and without consulting Olga, to an open-air museum of a romanticizable past. I ran the *büfé*, Olga said. Best years of my life. I was at the cinema every evening. Stop by my place sometime, I'll show you photos, she said, before awkwardly climbing onto her mended bicycle. I have so many photos from back then. I live just around the corner from here. Number 24.

Józsi was searching for a missing object from the cinema, he said, and that had led him to the little film splicer for repairing tears. For every object that's missing, I know who took it, he said. Evidently he kept an inventory list. Was it in his head? Or did he have an old piece of paper in one of his shop-counter drawers, where he for years had kept a list of missing things? I imagined Józsi sailing through the streets on his *Easy Rider* bicycle and showing up at certain houses. I saw him knocking on clattering yard gates or street-facing windows until someone appeared. He was very tall and might have intimidated some people if he showed up at their gate at dusk, talking about some half-forgotten petty theft. You couldn't even really call it a theft; an unauthorized taking, perhaps, but who should authorize anyone to take equipment from such a rundown place? One person or another might have laid claim to objects from the mysterious projection booth, while the projectors gathered dust, for weeks, for months, and the posters, unchanging in the display boxes, continued to reference days and months long past, and the front doors flickering gold remained shut, and the council workers, sent to the building every now and again, came in through the side entrance, from the yard. It was reached by way of a tremendous gate ostensibly much older than the cinema building itself; the pink paint peeled from the cracked wood, and the handle was positioned at a comfortable height for a giant to reach out and grab. It was a gate for horse-and-carriages, which way back in the past might have been accommodated in the cinema yard, where the owls now perched, their heads tucked below their wings all the day. Some curious worker, sent by the municipality, might have taken it when he was left alone in the cinema's many rooms, although it had nothing to do with his job; perhaps he was unable to withstand the temptation of such a mysterious object, and hoped that its function and applicability would reveal themselves to him at some point, once he possessed it; once it sat on his own workbench it would disclose its utility and perhaps even spread some of the vibrating lustre of the cinema's magic.

Regardless of what had motivated the individual purloiners to commit the deed, Józsi intuited their identity. As it turned out, his investigations proved him correct almost always, and below the shop counter he had accrued a store of regained objects, whose very existence and necessity for the cinema were entirely new to me. In addition to his inventory of missing things, he also began a list of things to acquire, and offered to write it all down for me, as if it was already a done deal and the revitalization of the cinema lay in our hands, his and mine. Most everything in this inventory, which first and foremost concerned replacement parts for the projectors and the

53

screen, was foreign to me as well. One hot July afternoon Józsi invited me to accompany him to the cinema. He had straightened up a bit: the film strips hung on a clothes hanger of sorts, the dead flies were swept into a black pile on a dustpan. In the midday summer light, the projectors stood like two sad, decommissioned animals, unfit and unwanted, yet in no position to search for a new place. Not even capable of lying down and dying. Józsi opened the side doors to the projectors' bellies and explained what to expect, to replace, to test for functionality. The entrails of a mythical creature revealed themselves, along with a hollow chamber of a considerable scale, large enough for an entire film to hide away in.

I could do little aside from nod; I saw the cinema before me in a strange evening radiance, attributable to the angle of the sun that time of year, streaming in the back window of the projection booth. It passed through the crowns of the old trees in the garden, their leaves casting shadows so much like hands, creating the illusion that they were waving, and as in my childhood I was then seized by the feeling that something was happening that I didn't understand, yet didn't want to miss a single second of. Later I explored the deep, overgrown yard while Józsi smoked by the back door. On the other side of the wall that separated the cinema garden from the police station grounds, I heard someone whispering, haggling with another person over a fine. I saw them as if before me, sensing the figures belonging to the voices: the one man had committed some offence, a petty theft—perhaps he'd even been caught in the act, in some dim corridor, still holding the empty wallet he'd stolen from a starving widow, or gripping a pig's trotter snatched from a freezer, hastily placed in the hall as it was being unloaded—and the other man, a police officer, who accepted his explanation as plausible, perhaps in the name of an old friendship or distant memories, and half-anxious, half-morose, would let it slide at the end of the conversation—of course not without a small IOU in return, whatever it was the delinquent had to offer. The sun went down, and the owls broke away from the crowns of the tall old walnut trees with a dark, quiet rustling of their pinions, first sinking below the branches where they had slept all day, then spreading their wings and rising higher, gliding through the air with a barely audible, gentle buzzing of the pinion feathers, before disappearing into the evening. Cinema birds. Or, *mozi* birds. Moving images in the guise of birds. In my mind I already saw people sitting on long wooden benches in the *mozi*'s outstretched yard, a film gliding across an open-air screen; it had to be a rapidly moving one, Dziga Vertov, for instance, with a wild sequence of images, faces, gestures, short scenes that opened up into something dazzling and utterly foreign here in this place, a freeing foreignness, from which you would then awake into a dulcet evening, cloaked in this melancholy emptiness and slowness.

Among the wonders of the cinema is its ability to interfere with the continuum of time for the duration of a film. The cinema partitions off, envelops, excludes all but what takes place on the screen, and within its four walls it creates a world that follows rules different from those left behind, outside the cinema. A new concept of time valid for the length of the film unfurls on the screen. This establishment of a separate space with its own rules is what distinguishes the cinema from other modes of watching films. The distance you have to overcome to reach it is part of this experience of a temporary dissolution of the rules of time and space, and you take this step willingly in order to expose yourself to a different, idiosyncratic space and become a part of it. Once you disregard the fact that a projected celluloid film delivers a different experience of light, space, colour and materiality than a digital copy or a video, then seeing a film on a personal screen is no different from seeing it in the cinema, as far as the plot, the characters, the story are concerned—yet the experience is fundamentally different, as it occurs without a partitioning off, without surmounting the distance between your trusted, domestic surroundings and the cinema, without the conscious act of entering into a space that is subjected to different rules and without animating the range between the eye and the projection surface. The cinema achieves a nesting of time, it infiltrates the fourth dimension. The cinema as a black box represents a wondrous container of time, which defies the course of seconds, minutes and hours during a film, questioning it in silence. A trip to the cinema expands the world and stretches time; the cinema remains a place of wonder.

In his workshop Józsi made me a copy of the cinema key, so I could come and go as I pleased. He also gave me an old bicycle which I was allowed to store there. Now it was August, and the groups of Hungarian-speaking Romanian children had been funnelled through the country of their native language; the owner of the lodging house reluctantly rented me a room, explaining that she would close for the season on 20 August. That was a national holiday, when, they said, every year summer came to a spectacular end. I rode the bicycle past the village limits, past the rustling fields of corn and sunflowers. Here and there were still large groups of poppies, stiff calyptras on bone-dry stems, the poppy seeds whispering inside, cracks extending down the grooved capsules, small black seeds fluttering out at the slightest breeze. Everything appeared to be desiccating away, lingering as it dried out, in order to make it easier for the harvesters when they came and separated the kernels, grains, seeds from the stems and chaff in a thick cloud of plant and soil dust.

I visited the cinema every day without coming any closer to knowing what I hoped to find there. For hours I sat on a seat in the viewing auditorium and observed the slow shifts of light falling through the high windows in the exit corridor. At Józsi's behest, three men brought over the screen from the communal administrative office, where it had been stored in a shed. They carried the long roll through the village and once they reached the cinema they told me that everyone had asked when it would reopen. Perhaps Józsi had instructed them to tell this story as well. They heaved the dirty roll onto the steps beside the coat check and then laid it on the thin strip of stage in front of the main auditorium wall. I watched them from the seating rows and wondered if I should understand their appearance as part of a theatre play or as a film rehearsal. After they left I struggled to unroll the canvas far enough to get a good idea of its condition. A surface rendered entirely useless came to light. The material had decomposed, it was cracked and brittle, the synthetic resin varnish covering the thin, woven-in metal parts had deteriorated, and small white fragments flaked off. In this state it now lay there, misappropriated and soiled, the piece that had acquiesced to countless images, and now had gone to ruin—due to what? Due to a lack, as with so many other things around? A lack of light, of images, of gazes? Or was it the residual light, images and gazes that had been rolled up along with the material, stuffed in and confined, abandoned to hopelessness between the layers, where they developed corrosive qualities? Every remnant is also a reference to something lost; in this sense, there were only two different angles from which to determine the extent of the damage.

Despite the August heat, the cinema was cool; several winters had left behind remains of frost and snow in the masonry walls, and even the direct beam of sunlight coming through the south-facing windows of the exit corridor didn't bring significant warmth into the rooms. I convinced myself that this coolness was the reason why I spent so much time there. I explored the small rooms and adjacent buildings, where old cinema seats were stored—parts of the previous wooden model that had served before the mustard-yellow cushions —as well as lamps, empty bulbous wine bottles and framed photos of film stars, few of whom I recognized. They bore Russian, Polish, Hungarian names, and two 'Westerners' were among them. Some of the photos were autographed. Had they arrived like that? Or had the actors visited? How might such a star-appearance have transpired? Did they pull up in elegant cars to a crowd of people waiting, all enthusiasm, holding pictures that they wanted to have signed? The autograph culture in socialist countries was renowned. I imagined the stars positioned on the stage in front of the screen, saying a few words to the audience either before or after the film, declaring their love of Hungary or even this particular place, which, after all, was the first town liberated by the Russians—perhaps there had even been a distant relative of the respective star among the soldiers?

Generations of spiders had woven webs around the photos, chairs, and enamelled signs affixed to the doors, indicating an office, a storage room, men's and women's toilets, the projection booth. One sign read: Risk of death!

That evening, after the screen was delivered, I bumped into Józsi in front of the cinema. He was taking an evening stroll with his wife. Józsi's wife was named Ljuba and she was from Kyiv. She was even taller than Józsi and had the air of a resolute sportswoman, although in his presence she seemed to go out of her way to assume a slight hunch, which vanished as soon as he was gone. She had come to town many years ago as a Russian language teacher and fallen in love with the film projectionist, after a thunderstorm interrupted the screening of one of her favourite films and the two of them had patiently waited it out together in the foyer of the dark cinema. She practically had the cinema to herself for this romantic Russian film, she explained, and she was very thankful for the projectionist's company during the blustering storm, and so began their love story, which had already endured several decades. Józsi nodded affirmatively. At the time a lightning bolt hit one of the projectors, and they had to wait for two weeks for a specialist from Budapest to come and replace the damaged fuse. Every day he waited for the technician in the cinema, whose telephone had also been struck by lightning, and every day Ljuba passed by to ask whether the technician had come, whether the projectors were up and running again, whether the interrupted film would be continued.

I watched the two of them walk down the street at dusk. Two giants, growing ever smaller on their way to the horizon, and it occurred to me I had forgotten to ask which film it was that Ljuba loved so much and that had found no other audience.

Shortly before 20 August I ran across Zoran. He treated me to an ice cream; Erzsébet Cukrászda had recently opened her newly ornate doors just around the corner from the cinema. Parked on the small street-facing terrace was a colourful cargo bicycle with bells and a sunshield, which an employee with a somewhat mousy face took out in the afternoons, riding through the town streets, ringing bells, squeezing the trumpet horn and occasionally calling out loudly to lure inhabitants from their closed gardens and houses, in order to sell them ice cream from coolers. It had been a while since I'd seen Zoran and I was already hoping he had given up the idea of the cinema changing hands. But no: With his ice cream spoon he pointed at a ranch house a few metres down the street, on the same side as the ice cream shop. There, he said, there is the solicitor who will draw up the contract. It's a good price, he added. You can trust me. Then he told me, casually, about his brain tumour, which he wanted to have operated on in the United States. He used an old-fashioned word to reference the tumour: a growth. It was a word they used in my childhood—not a bad word to describe the insatiable hunger of a tumour. Zoran cupped his hands to form a cavity to explain the growth to me. He slid the cavity around the table and assured me there was nothing malignant in his head, and his gestures almost had an air of tenderness, his gaze resting amiably on the tumour represented by his cupped hands.

In August evening came early. Dusk was short, the light retreating from the vastness which shimmered in the heat, murky with dust; at first the horizon was a streaky brown in the south and the east, as if a storm were approaching, but it proved to be nothing more than the gathering evening, followed by night. In August there were no longer pleasant fragrances, only the very mild smell of soil and decay from between the pavement and the street, where unharvested fruit oozed into the ground, fermenting, and the smell of dust. Everything leaned low, pressed to the ground by summer. Here and there in the late afternoon women met to sit on benches in front of their yard gates and talk. That's when I came across Olga again, who waved me over. She lived in a small box house built in the post-war style, and through her open gate I made out a glass veranda full of plants. The bench in front of Olga's house was very high and the old women swung their legs. Olga's legs were stuck in the laced boots, which had heels of varying heights, as I now saw. This is our new cinema director, Olga introduced me to her acquaintances, who nodded apprehensively. You'll need a house, Olga said, and pointed to the yellow house across the street. That one's empty. A nice house, a nice house, the other women murmured affirmatively. Then we'll be neighbours, and I'll tell you about the cinema. I've got a lot to say. Olga nodded, as if to communicate, You can go now, I've finished. I walked a large circle back to the lodging house. Someone stood by the river, attempting to fish in the small stream. I met Józsi and Ljuba on their evening stroll. We heard you're going to buy the cinema, Ljuba said. Józsi grinned like a child. It's about time we have a cinema again. When are you going to the solicitor? Soon, I said. Definitely soon.

Leaving Budapest was not easy. From the distance of two-hundred-and-thirty kilometres the decaying cinema in a half-abandoned village that purported to have once been a big town seemed less enchanted and in need of a revival than it had in person. The cinemas I had access to in the vicinity of my apartment, with their smooth projection screens and functioning projectors, the life of the city and not least the courtyard theatre bore more weight than

I had realized while I was in the south-east, in the presence of the *mozi*. Despite the forecast, the last days of August and the beginning of September were extremely hot. A certain tired displeasure hung over the flea market, the offering of beautiful items seemed depleted, the merchant Feri chirred wearily through his artificial voice box, and I couldn't understand what he said. In the background his slow-witted daughters were painting their fingernails for a night of dancing. On the way home from the cemetery, where she went once a year to visit the grave of her deceased husband, Julika had suffered a heart attack and remained in the hospital for a few days. Then one morning she came back, at dawn, the hospital gown visible beneath the smock she had worn to the cemetery, and she explained that a strange restlessness had compelled her to come home. Later that day a nearby building with a construction similar to ours collapsed, just like that, as if brushed the wrong way by a breath of late-summer wind, and it was all anyone could talk about for days, especially as the dust it had whirled up hung around the alleys, as if it didn't know where else to go.

Julika seemed lighter now than before her heart attack, buoyant almost, with a spring to her step that seemed to nearly propel her in the air as she brushed past her geraniums, removing wilted leaves and stems. I told her about the large abandoned cinema that had been closed for so long. Ah, the cinema. She gestured with her hand as if throwing something away. Why bother with the cinema any more. It's a place of obsolete passions. As a young woman she had taken a cinema-rogue for a sweetheart, Like no one else, that one, she said. She chased after his shirttails, but one day it was over for her. He had nothing but the cinema in his head. He was a good-looking man, too, Julika said, rolling back her eyes, as if she could still see him up there in front of her, behind her eyelids. But she was no match for the cinema, so one day she packed her things, returned to Budapest, and married the postman. He was as good as the cinema man was handsome. It was my dream to become an artistic gymnast, she said, but I threw in the towel for the cinema man. And when I got back from the lowlands, it was as if my joints had fallen asleep. First I worked in the spinning mill, out on Csepel, then as a seamstress in the shirt factory—we were all girls, and there was always something to laugh about. Later they gave us our own sewing machines so we could also work from home. I always liked going there; back then in the evenings my husband still worked as an electrician—for dollars—after he was finished with his day job, and eventually we saved enough money to buy a television; at the time hardly anyone had one. From every side and above and below, the neighbours peered in our windows just as soon as we switched on the television. I distinctly felt their eyes, even though we always sat facing away from the window. So maybe it was a bit like the cinema for them, except that they couldn't hear anything. Nothing but silent films. What do you want to go to the cinema for, I would say to my husband whenever he suggested it. That's what the television's for. But Laci, I never got him off my mind, him and his passion. And the cinema in general. The way it always went dark before the film. The people, all these dark heads, all of them looking, all in the same direction, as if under a spell. That was something else altogether. But I was happy.

In the evenings when I went to the cinema I paid attention to details and fixtures: The differences between the old-fashioned tear-off tickets made of a thin textured cardboard and the smooth ones printed from a computer; the positioning of the ticket taker; the lighting and the signs. I anxiously realized that in the future I would be reliant on my own programme, which would be available for a week and, needless to say, should also please the local audience, who after spending years in front of a television, without a cinema, had certainly lost sight of many things that had once been visible—and above all, forgotten *how* to see them. They had weaned themselves off everything exceptional about looking out from a silent community of nameless figures in the dark.

Ildikó came to do hair for the last time; she was going to marry her boyfriend with the black curls in Bulgaria, and change jobs. She had the tourism industry in mind, she explained, and I imagined her working as a receptionist and hair stylist at a hotel by the Black Sea, and in that moment, suddenly and for no apparent reason I remembered a barbershop I once saw in Vidin, the Bulgarian town on the Danube River, where early one morning three men with frothy chins sat in a row in old red salon chairs, all three leaning back their heads, and at the time it appeared to me, for reasons I no longer understand, as if they were preparing to film an execution scene. Everything seemed suspended in expectation of the camera.

I told no one in Budapest of my plans and put off my move. It was a mild, beautiful autumn, and I walked through the city districts into the outskirts, discovering along the way little workshops and basement shops, heading east on roads that abruptly ended in a pastoral-suburban territory, where the asphalt slowly petered out and between piles of tires, junkyards and paint shops goats grazed the thin grass, and the last leaves rustled in the poplars. Every few weeks I drove to the south-east, wandered around the cinema, moved things here and there, always discovering something new: an additional closet, additional photographs of forgotten actors, additional objects whose function eluded me. I conferred with Józsi, who was contemplating a solution for the main wall, and furnished the house across the street from Olga sufficiently to live there. Olga waved to me from her bench when I cleaned away the fly corpses that had accumulated between the glass panes of the box-type windows, and she brought me over a tablecloth with embroidered fairy-tale scenes: her school graduation handwork. She offered to sell me an accordion and a wobbly green plant stand. I purchased the plant stand; I could not play the accordion. Later Olga told me it had once belonged to her sweetheart, the man she moved to town for. They had both waited tables in a tavern by the Danube River, in former Yugoslavia, and her colleague had also provided musical entertainment on the accordion. It was in fact the sound of his accordion that had sparked her love, and she followed him to this place without even asking what drew him here. Since the cinema was located across the street from the restaurant where he played, alternating with, in her words, a well-loved 'gypsy ensemble', it seemed to her the obvious choice to look for a job there. For years she stood behind the cinema *büfé*, selling coffee, *traubisoda*, and cheese-curd pastries. In autumn they procured a large, electric aluminium vat to heat corn on the cob, the snack offered in colder months. In the cinema we were always warm, she said; first we had the large, tiled stove in the foyer, then came the convection heating. It was always snug. I remained in the *büfé* for the duration of the film, as well. That way I could hear Karli's accordion from across the street and the film from the auditorium, the voices and sounds and music, and I had my own thoughts about it and imagined things. I only started watching the films after Karli was gone. One day he died while playing, late in the evening, while I waited for him in the *büfé*. He just slumped over, resting his head on the accordion, which produced a long, strange sound, like a sigh or a lament. I heard it all the way from the cinema *büfé* and I knew right away something wasn't right—that's how greatly this new, unprecedented sound ripped at my heart. After that I always sat in the auditorium and watched the film, so I wouldn't have to hear the music from across the street. Then the gypsy ensemble played every day—they played beautifully, you had to give it to them—but it was no comparison to Karli's accordion. Before the film and during the breaks I switched on the radio. Otherwise I wouldn't have been able to stand it. But the films—I really grew to like them. Never would I have thought the cinema could be such a rock in my life; every film was like an excursion into another country, every time, and I was alone and at the same time I wasn't. Just wait till I get home and tell Karli about this, I often thought when the suspense was high, but then I would remember that he was gone. But the cinema, I really loved it to the last. It was a sad day when it closed.

She stowed away Karli's accordion in the large cabinet on the front side of her glass veranda. It stood beside a pair of very large, pointy black men's shoes which, I assumed, had also been Karli's.

In November the weather in Budapest took a turn for the worse. An overcast sky, thin rain, and once even a wet snow fell, melting immediately. The courtyard theatre, which had already grown lethargic after Ildikó's departure, fell asleep entirely. Julika was the only one I still saw, when she stood outside and smoked—even after her heart attack, she didn't quit. Inside her apartment the television flickered, the voices and the music reaching the corridor outside; Julika seemed harder of hearing than before. Even on these cool days she didn't pull socks over her scaly, blue-veined feet, instead slipping on the same mules that she wore in summer. Of late she had acquired some mischievous quality, as if inside she were perpetually laughing about something no one else could know about, her eyes twinkling like two little lamps behind the thick glasses, winking occasionally as if in secret agreement and quietly chuckling, cackling; occasionally, if the janitor's loud snores woke me up, I thought I heard her issue sharp little whistles, perhaps intended for the sparrows, or the surly winter blackbirds. How's life down there in the lowlands, she asked me one evening. Have you found a pumpkin yet, to stand on and wave from?

III. Interlude

...the tires are whirring on the wet asphalt
like the apparatus in the cinematograph.
—FRANZ KAFKA

IN MARCH 1927, Deutsch Laszló, known as Laci, gained employ-
ment in the timber trade. Laci had trained as a merchant and could
already write elegantly and compile neat lists; he was a meticulous
dresser, maintained an immaculately groomed moustache and
enjoyed standing at the handsome lectern in the office. One day in
late May, Laci's employer asked him to accompany him the following
week on a trip to Budapest, for a business meeting with a wholesaler.
Laci's mother brushed out by hand his best clothing, as well as his
genteel hat, and at dawn he made his way through the streets, heading for the train station. Day broke and a matte light fell through
the window shafts of the tobacco sheds along the tracks. The sun
rose at the very moment the train arrived and as Laci stepped in
behind the timber merchant it felt nearly ceremonious. They
chugged across the flatland in the morning light, passing blossoming
acacias, cornfields and cherry orchards, crooked village houses and
tall grain mills and yellow train stations, and over the Tisza River,
which Laci had never seen before, with protuberant bushes lining
its banks. The timber merchant rested his head on the red curtains

89

of the partition window and slept, while Laci contemplated in silent excitement the infinite vastness of the landscape and felt his heart pounding in his throat, while outside the houses, standing ever closer together, the factories and the shop yards, the woven tracks of the freight yards, the laundries and the cab yards and the multitudes of people in motion signalled that they were approaching the capital. The timber merchant awoke, smoothed his jacket and vest with his hands, pulled out his pocket watch and glanced at it; the train had arrived on time. They exited at Józsefváros Station. His eyes wandering in every direction, Laci occasionally stumbled as they walked down cobblestone streets among maids, tradesmen and running children. Beggars crossed their path, itinerant women merchants thrust at them their wares, carried on the portable shops they transported on their bodies above their stomachs, the smell of strudel wafting from small booths between the buildings. The multistorey buildings on both sides gave way to two-, then one-storey houses resembling those in Laci's hometown, and the cobblestones petered out into a dusty ground deeply furrowed by wagon wheels. The road, more accurately a lane, was lined by workshops, construction yards, stores of rusty iron and weather-beaten wood, worn-down tires, frames, tools, so many objects all dreaming of a new utility. A meagre slice of meadow opened up, goats grazing on it. Poplars lined the path, but swathes of linden scent also wafted in the air: it was May and lindens were never far off. In the distant freight yard locomotives whistled.

In the wholesaler's yard Laci had a difficult time following the conversation, since the two men spoke German, of which he had only a rudimentary knowledge, and, making matters worse, the wholesaler slid his cigar back and forth in his mouth as he spoke, all the while gesticulating. They were talking about lumber and delivery times and prices, and Laci's employer nodded in agreement, taking notes in an order book, and occasionally he asked a question. After they had crossed the timber yard and Laci, imitating his employer, had run his fingertips over the raw, reddish-orange cut surface of this or that log, corrugated from the blade of the saw, without feeling any essential difference in the quality of the wood, he was dismissed for several hours of free time in the city, while the two timber merchants proceeded to their meal.

Laci followed the tram tracks back to the city, past the one-storey, then two-storey houses, and the four- and five-storey buildings with balconies, past community gardens, past a market and shops with goods on display, until finally he reached the ring road. He looked right and left into the deep yards that opened up behind the gates and stopped to examine a few display boxes with photographs, above all the photographs of actresses, all of whom were beautiful—had anyone asked, he wouldn't have been able to decide who was the most beautiful. At last, after taking a particularly long gander at the pictures in a display box on the magnificent Erzsébet körút, Laci pulled out his wallet and counted his money. Then he went to the cinema.

Laci knew films. At village celebrations and carnival festivities they screened films in tents, or in the open air, projected onto masonry walls; moving pictures, short episodes, mostly designed to make you laugh or shudder with fear, accompanied by the projector's whir, and warped by the uneven wall or wrinkles in the surface of the tent. The people in these short films moved quickly and awkwardly, and their haste in play as well as in terror took the viewers' breath away—how quickly it turns, the world streaming from the projector! And what a world it is! Dust danced in the machine's beam of light, and when the film ended, some people approached the wall and ran their hands along the plaster or the cloth tent, searching for remnants of the images. During the screenings occasionally a reader stood beside the projection surface and read aloud the intertitles for anyone who couldn't keep up, but generally it was much too loud to understand them. There were accompanying musicians, piano and accordion players who occasionally became drunk, and it often ended in skirmishes which got lost in the general excitement. It was a pleasure for each and every one: they slapped their thighs, laughing at the protagonist's mishaps, and let out a deep sigh whenever the film ended with two lovers, the wooing hero and his wooed heroine, standing cheek to cheek, ideally accentuated by a bouquet of flowers, before disappearing in the contracting round image, as if they were being pulled away into a tunnel by a strange force, leaving behind nothing but darkness. Yet if you remained seated for a while, or returned to the tent of moving pictures throughout the course of carnival, you could watch the same episode again from the beginning, since it resided on a reel that could be placed on the projector and played again and again. As a boy, Laci had once asked a projectionist why the film always begins, correctly, at the beginning, despite the fact that after the film ran its course the beginning must have been at the start of the reel. If I give the players enough time, the projectionist said, they all resume their places in the film in the correct order. They just need a bit of time. He winked at Laci, and Laci winked back, bemused, and throughout the evening he periodically glanced over at the reels leaning on the wall, hoping to detect a movement, but it was in vain. In Budapest he now sat, not on a backless bench, crammed between other people who stomped their feet and flailed their arms, but in a seat—admittedly not in one of the pricy cushioned rows, but still, it was a seat—and like a well-brought up boy he placed his hat on his knees and followed the long, tragic arc of the film, which was presented here on a smooth, flawless surface, punctuated by frequent short pauses, an elegant lady accompanying the plot with her piano music.

It was a long, sad film, much longer than the other films that Laci knew. At the end there was a large fire, and even if they did manage to save a child, how should life go on? Laci remained in his seat, stunned, as if he had stepped into another life, and then he took a look around, saw the other viewers leave the auditorium while quietly pattering, and he searched for the projectionist.

When Laci stepped out of the cinema onto the ring street, it was already dark. He was dizzy from the films he'd seen, and from silently observing the projectionist's hand movements. For a moment Laci had placed his hand on the vibrating projector and thought: the quiver of life. The evening air was heady with the scent of linden blossoms, people sauntered in the light of the streetlamps, automobiles passed down the boulevard, and everything seemed livelier now, by night, than it had by day, and you could even buy flowers, single roses or small bound bouquets. Laci struggled to find his way back to the station, where the last train home was already long departed. He sat on a hard wooden bench on the platform and let all he had seen and learnt at the cinema sink in: the film itself, flying off the reel, the large machine through which it passed, aided by a number of tiny spindles, the smooth film whose edges he had carefully felt, the teeny images on the film material that then became so incomprehensibly gigantic on screen. The projectionist might have treated him like a child, but he was nice and explained a thing or two in the longer pause between the screenings. Laci had taken him for the cinema owner and listened, practically frozen with admiration, which nevertheless did not fade once the projectionist had cleared up the misunderstanding: It takes a great deal of money to own a cinema in such a refined location, he said, he was merely the projectionist, the guy who knew his way around the machines, whereas the owner was chauffeured over every evening, in order to count the day's profits while smoking a cigar. But one day, he, the projectionist, would have his own cinema somewhere, perhaps in a big town. After all, every town will need a cinema at some point, he said. A cinema! Laci thought, sitting on the hard train station bench, while a small thunderstorm brewed overhead in the night sky. He dreamed he was master of projectors, upholstered seating and a flawless screen, while the rain, accompanied by a distant roll of thunder, began to drum on the roof of the train platform.

In 1927 Budapest had over a hundred cinemas. Although it was no longer the same dazzling attraction it had been prior to the First World War, no other pastime enjoyed greater popularity with the masses, and many cinemas offered a new film daily. Countless musicians made their living as accompaniments to silent films, countless young women took poorly paid work as ushers and ticket saleswomen, and everyone wanted to bask in the screen's glowing reflection. Film was incessantly exposed and developed, the strand of celluloid never tore, feeding dreams, lending visions, opening eyes, allowing people to experience a vastness never there before, and talkies resounded on the horizon. Everyone wanted to visit the cinema, to sit staring, all in the same direction, all together. The cinema beckoned the world into the dark room and then radiated beyond its limits, in the eyes that had all seen across the distance to the horizon of the screen; the pace of the film determined the pace of life, and word became image and paragon, leaving its mark on people. Whoever sat at the lever of the projector could adjust the speed of the world at whim, whether as a ruse or accidentally, helpless victim to the mood of a machine, while the public wavered between terror and amazement. The cinema was the world.

Laci Deutsch was no longer satisfied by his work for the timber merchant, even after the ill humour occasioned by his disappearance in Budapest had dissipated. Even the new typist, who operated the recently arrived typewriter, concluded definitively that Laci spent too much time looking out the window—where there was nothing to see aside from the street that ran through the big town. The timber merchant was located on a long, straight road, and if you walked out the gate, to the west you could see the small attendant's hut in front of the train station, and to the east you saw all the way to the post office at the intersection that marked approximately the centre of town. For the life of her, the typist could not understand what out there had him so mesmerized, since she too saw and heard the horse-and-carriages coming from the train station, the two-wheeled cargo bicycles of the onion and garlic merchants heading east from Makó, as well as the lumbering wine barrels positioned on the beds of the carts emerging from the hills beyond Arad, which occasionally stood out against the eastern horizon in the palest of

95

blues, like a child's clumsy drawing, and the honking automobiles that passed through town seldom and loudly, and yet she couldn't imagine what about any of this might be interesting. She was familiar with the stench of the Makó onion merchant, did not drink wine, rarely travelled by train and was waiting in vain for an invitation to ride in an automobile, and yet Laci Deutsch, as she well knew, had recently obtained a driver's license and on Sundays chauffeured the town's wealthy men and women. He had even made it all the way to Temesvár and Szeged. He was a good driver, the people said, and they forgave him when he came too late, trotting out of the closest cinema, where he had forgotten both the time and his clients.

Laci looked outside ever more frequently, for longer, more askew. If he tilted his head, he could see through the gap between two houses, to the opposite side of the street, and all the way to the horizon, as if the subsequent rows of houses were intentionally laid out like this, to afford a view into the vastness. One day he glanced at the clock even more often than he peered into this splinter of vastness. That morning from the window he'd seen the covered wagon roll past and read the ornate lettering on its side: Motion pictures on the move! The cinema is coming to you!

Laci knew the driver of the travelling cinema, who regularly came to the area to screen new films, accompanied by a girl named Erzsike, who wore her hair in a bun secured by a pearl-encrusted bow and on a harmonium played melodies which generally got lost in the laughter and mutterings of the crowd. On his lunch break Laci found the wagon parked in its usual place by the river, where at other times poultry was bought and sold. The horses were grazing and

Imre, the travelling cinema's owner, appeared sullen. His musician had walked off with a conjurer hired to entertain the audience between screenings, a nimble-fingered man who knew how to make a thing or two disappear—in this case, Erzsike. And he, Imre, wasn't able to manage both the music and the projector. The dissatisfaction was already palpable in the villages he had visited in the previous weeks; the laughter, even if it normally would have drowned out the music, seemed thin, and nothing was as it should have been. Laci requested to operate the projector that evening. After work he learned all the necessary hand movements and was feverish with excitement for the first run, while Imre took a stab at the harmonium. An audience gathered, the evening was humid, the air stood still, and everyone spoke of longing for a storm and dabbed their foreheads with handkerchiefs. Laci carefully slid a piece of film through his fingertips, feeling the smoothness of the material, but also the sharp edges of the punched holes that the teeth of the projector would grab on to. He held the strip up to the light and, despite the oppressive heat, felt a chill run down his spine as he realized that he himself was the one who would rouse these little images into moving scenes that would make the viewers' skulls, with their hair variously coifed and styled, appear small as the heads of flies.

In the hot tent, sweat drenched his collar as he delivered to the screen scenes of hope, disappointment, depravity, greed and wicked endings, as well as cheer and happy endings, all the product of coincidence. Standing at the projector, the weight of the screening on his shoulders, he felt more removed from the film, since he could discern the figures on the lower edge of the picture, crammed closely together on the viewing benches in a permanent state of disquiet, and at the same time he felt closer to it than he would have from the audience, since he was also able to touch the film with his hands and generally considered himself necessary for its apparition. Meanwhile, Imre's uncertain fingers slowly became familiar with the harmonium's keys.

That Saturday evening the lovers gathered at the entrance for the last screening. A wind had picked up outside, eddying the dust on the dry, hard-packed dirt ground, forming small funnels with little things swirling helplessly inside: small pieces of wood, scraps of twine, the scattered, used entry tickets from previous screenings. Thunder rumbled in the distance, frogs croaked in the rushes along the small river and the heady scent of the last linden blossoms seemed to blanket everything in a film, sweet and at the same time vile with its slightly rotten tack. By the time the audience was let in, the partition featuring a romantic film poster had already been blown over by the wind a dozen times, Imre having picked it up just as often, and after everyone took their seats Imre assured them they were about to see one of the most modern films of all, while the whistling of the wind picked up outside in the background and the roll of thunder moved notably closer. Of all, he repeated for emphasis, as the light in the tent turned off and the black-and-white snow flickered, crackling on the screen, thus beginning the film.

For a time, romantic entanglements distracted people from acknowledging the thunder, the howling wind and even the dazzling flashes of lighting which pierced the cracks and holes in the tent, but then a cold gust of wind blew in, upsetting the tarpaulin at the entrance, and with a deafening drumming, rain set in. The girls shrieked and, seeking shelter, turned to their clueless accompaniments, who began to fear for the elegance of their moustaches, faced with the deluge of water from the sky. Before long water penetrated the tent; Laci Deutsch had the presence of mind to snatch the film reels from the folding table, where they sat beside the projector, and when, beneath the brunt of the rain, the tent's crown also developed small tears, letting in the water, he threw himself over the projector, which thankfully was not yet warm, refusing to surrender it to the storm, while a number of couples plunged into the bluster of the storm with pointed cries and husky curses, for fear of being buried beneath a collapsing tent.

But the tent did not collapse. The wet panels of cotton duck clapped limply in the flagging wind, the downpour gave way to a steady murmur, the roll of thunder receded and the lightning strikes became rare, then ceased altogether.

Laci remained the travelling cinema's projectionist. He left behind the timber trade and his family home, heading off with Imre in the cinema wagon, stopping in outlying towns and villages. Imre perfected the art of playing the harmonium to accompany a film so fully that a certain reputation preceded them, and for a while it even worked as a charm to protect them from the large shadow cast by the sound film, which required a different set of skills and equipment. Business flourished such that they were able to trade in their horse-and-cart for an automobile with a covered cargo bed, which allowed them to clatter into even the most remote villages. Eventually, however, the audience stayed home, regardless of the unprecedented noises Imre elicited from his harmonium with nimble fingers, and despite the dexterity Laci demonstrated in projecting film, occasionally also repairing it with breathtaking agility. The audience demanded sound films. After purchasing the automobile, Imre was strapped too thin to acquire any additional equipment, and so they split ways in a city called Székesfehérvár, which boasted a radio station with a tower. They found a place to park in a tavern yard, where they were also given permission to screen in a drafty building attached to the back of the dining room. Their final presentation took place on a rainy Saturday evening. Laci initially wanted to screen the last film they had that was still intact, which lay neatly wound on reels in a large box and told the heart-wrenching story of a young woman who became involved in a police investigation, but then he decided against it. Maybe he didn't want to risk damaging the reels, since they had to be sent back, or maybe he suspected that they would draw an audience who sought to get out of the evening drizzle more than they longed for a view of the screen. He opened the box where he kept the film odds and ends he had saved over the course of years, when segments of a film were so decayed or damaged that a coherent screening was no longer possible. Laci had a great predilection for the smooth celluloid strips with their variously coated sides, these bands of material in which images and movements only appeared to sleep, as if they believed themselves salvaged and entrusted to his care. On the spur of the moment he spliced together enough film strips for a generous half-hour; it was, after all, a gratis screening. He didn't even pay attention to what he was montaging, focusing instead only on the precision of his handwork, and then he carefully rolled the cobbled-together film onto a reel and announced his programme to Imre. In the misty evening twilight, about a dozen viewers gathered around, some with a beer stein in hand, a timid young couple situated on the rearmost seats. Laci fired up the projector, and he was gripped by a tremendous melancholy when he thought this might actually be the last film he would ever project. Imre gave it his best, playing a heart-warming repertoire, interspersed with short passages of galloping-horse sound effects, while Laci's view of the screen became clouded by tears, his work of chance rolling on as a complete oeuvre, containing his life, bearing the title *film*. Once it had run its course, only the young couple remained sitting, nestled cheek to cheek on the back chairs, their gazes glued to the projection screen, scarcely able to slip away from the rapture of looking and re-enter the reality of their surroundings without a film.

That evening Laci got drunk on sour wine, while Imre held a long monologue on the bleak future of the travelling cinema and the cinema in general, since a world with radio towers would eradicate the cinema, literally eradicate it, Imre repeated several times, speaking in a rage and altogether forgetting his wine. The cinema will decay like an old, fragile, foul-smelling piece of film, he concluded. When Laci awoke the next day on a plank bed in a tavern room, head pounding, he realized that Imre had left with the automobile and everything inside it. He settled accounts, paying his bed and bar tab, and on his way to the train station Laci felt a meagre stack of bills in his trouser pocket.

Budapest had changed. The bustle had given way to a universal oppression; on every street corner beggars extended their hands for alms and hungry children wailed; a restlessness was building in the factory yards around the low huts of the workers' tenements, and moustachioed policemen escorted through the streets not individual rogues but entire hordes of scabby faced have-nots who sought to organize a collective resistance to a prospective eviction from their homes or the loss of their livelihoods, or who simply were caught furtively helping themselves to spoiled vegetables between market stands. Above all, there were fewer cinemas. Laci trudged from one to another. They all showed talkies and a repertoire Laci was not yet familiar with. At first the voices seemed strange and artificial to him, but then he became accustomed to them. Occasionally there was a delay between sound and image, meaning the words spoken didn't match the lip movements, the facial expressions, the people. It occasionally made Laci laugh, then it annoyed him again, and in the end, he found it interesting. At every cinema, when the film ended, Laci would inquire about work. He would do any job, he assured them, even usher. That earned him suspicious glances; there were no male ushers. What did he have in mind? He was out of luck. No one invited him into the projection booth to take a look at the projectors, to say nothing of touching them, or to look through the narrow window into the auditorium. Laci spent all the money he had left on a somewhat greasy Borsalino hat from a second-hand market and accepted a position as a driver for a commercial laundry in Buda. Laci became familiar with every corner of the city as he delivered bundles of clean, starched and ironed wash wrapped in packing paper, and collected marked sacks of dirty laundry and brought them back to the cleaner. He saw hordes of people lining up for work, thronging in front of the public authorities, rushing into the turmoil on the street; he saw uniformed men, sometimes using their batons, and men in tattered clothing who walked quicker than the cars drove; he saw barricaded windows and broken windows, locked-up theatres and cinemas and the markets for the havenots, where they traded broken and damaged goods. On pleasant summer evenings he saw the sooty roofs of houses on the outskirts of town, men scrambling and jockeying for food to feed their loved ones, and tired shunting engines on cargo tracks; he saw musicians busking at courtyard entrances, barefoot children who stole from the apple ladies, and in the rearmost yard of a workshop for medical equipment, where once a week he delivered freshly laundered smocks, he watched a group of artistic gymnasts practicing with devotion, as if some single, double, triple flip might, with practise, catapult them out of the misery of the streets. Sometimes he took a short break there to watch a slender young girl practise jumps. She was able to lift herself into the air in such a wondrous way, her arms waving gently, so it briefly appeared as if she had wings. In the same street as the workshop for medical equipment and the courtyard corner with the artistic gymnasts, there was a one-storey building which always caught Laci's eye, because on the crumbling façade was the word *csillag*, written in iron letters that bled rust and just barely hung onto the anchorage. When driving by Laci never failed to inspect the lettering and wonder if the letters had slipped any farther.

One Sunday in autumn his search for a room led him to precisely this street, where apparently there were accommodations for rent. In amazement, he realized that the office clerk at the commercial laundry had scribbled down on a piece of paper the address of precisely the *csillag* building. The courtyard gate was open, and as he stood at the entrance his gaze fell directly onto a showcase with a pitted wooden frame; below the dirty glass he recognized still photographs from films and a portrait of an actress with yearning in her eyes, whose name was Lili and whom he had discovered only recently in the Budapest cinemas. He was offered a tiny room with a small stove, a table and a chair. He would have to find a bed for himself. The landlord was a nervous man in his fifties who wore a somewhat shabby fur coat too heavy and warm for the season and pointy black shoes, and he smoked without pause. He was going abroad, not entirely of his own volition, and he needed someone to watch over his property. He examined Laci. By property he meant the shuttered cinema. The Csillag was the gem of the neighbourhood, he said: it wasn't called *star* for nothing. Now he had to leave it in the lurch. He needed someone to live there, to make sure it didn't end up in the wrong hands. He had Laci at the word *cinema*. From that moment Laci was prepared to sculpt his own personal history and skills accordingly, in order to increase his chances of success and gain the owner's favour. Before Laci went so far as to tell a lie, the owner pulled out his keys and waved him into a dark room, which happened to be the cinema hall. He proceeded a few steps ahead, climbing up to the projection booth, where there were two massive projectors, larger than Laci had ever imagined a projector could be, and potbellied, as if they'd devoured several films along with their cast-and-crews. In a side closet it reeked acidic, like old celluloid. Laci was familiar with this smell, emanated by the material when it was too old, had been played too often, subjected to extreme fluctuations in temperature. Perhaps there was something salvageable in the box of reels and strips; his fingers began to quiver at the thought.

Laci was given the room, the keys, access to the projection booth. The owner shook his hand and gave him his thanks. Stern Ábel was his name. Deutsch László, Laci said, unsure whether to shake his hand again or salute him—a strange hesitation, as there was nothing militant about their exchange.

The route from his new apartment to work was long and diverse. Laci crossed the city every morning and every evening, passing through worlds where everything imaginable was for sale, from worn-down enamel bowls, whose revenue might fetch a piece of bread, to drops that made one's eyes glitter seductively. Sometimes on his way home he would stop at the cinema, but the screens seemed to be growing narrower, and the images less vast. The girls at the commercial laundry sang songs from romance films and counted their meagre pengő from a week's work, hoping by the third or fourth time to discover that it was enough, after all, for a ticket to see a film with Katalin Karády, the romantic heroine of the day. Laci was consumed by the thought of fixing up the Csillag Cinema. He had examined the projectors and painstakingly sorted the film strips, winding them onto reels. Most of the film strips were useless, brittle and sticky, and whenever Laci was exposed to the smell for a longer period of time he grew dizzy, and he could not say if it was because of the chemicals they released or merely the idea of disintegrated and disfigured images. He carried the box outside to the courtyard and set it down on the wall. In the rearmost corner of the courtyard was a walnut tree. The leaves were falling, although it wasn't autumn; although it was summer, a brown, wilted edge formed on every leaf, eating its way inward. Were I to film the tree now, Laci thought, later I could say: That was the autumn of such-and-such year, when

I lived in the Csillag Cinema. That's how it is with film, Laci thought. Film becomes reality. Or at any rate, the truth.

Bitter days arrived. Uniformed men multiplied like flies, every day there were brawls, and hungry children recognized a gun in every piece of wood they found and ambushed one another. Their screeching bullets zipped mournfully through the air, and after every such shouted exchange of fire the children were even hungrier than before. Meanwhile, the films in the cinemas grew louder, with marching music and traditional costumes, the girls with dewy eyes below their flower crowns, and Katalin Karády sang 'Somewhere in Russia'. Laci had been prudent enough to order a fake identity document in good time, in the name of the invalid Német Lajos, born in Transdanubia. He grew accustomed to the name, yet always felt like a counterfeit bill when he thought about how the new papers listed his birthplace in the foothills, and not in the plains. The office clerk at the commercial laundry accepted the name change in silence. One day, when he was out delivering a package to the workshop for medical devices, the slender artistic gymnast approached him and asked when the Csillag Cinema would reopen. She flashed her eyes at him, making him very bashful, and he said: Soon. Definitely soon.

It became advisable for Laci to quit his job, and he spent his days in the cinema. The artistic gymnast knocked at the door until he cautiously opened. She introduced herself as Julika and offered to help put the auditorium in order. Together they swept the floor and wiped down the seats, on which no one had sat for a long time. A broom in hand, Julika took a standing jump and brushed spiderwebs from the corners. In the courtyard she shook out the curtains, from which moths flew, and Laci boldly promised her a trial screening for next week. In the end it had to be postponed: Julika, who advertised sparkling eyedrops on a commercial street in the centre of town, where she stood jammed between two pieces of bottle-shaped pasteboard equipped with an eye slit, was indeed able to make her pupils glitter and glisten, yet occasionally the sparkling drops caused her burning distortions and veils, which clouded her gaze. While her eyes healed Laci recounted to her a number of films he knew, and she swore she could see it all in front of her, as if she were at the cinema. Laci didn't believe her, particularly in view of the fact that he often forgot small details, which he later added; then he would say: Now we have to change the reel, or: Now the projector needs to cool off a moment, or: Now for the intertitle, but he felt as if everything visible were running down between the words. A few weeks later Laci turned on the projectors, Julika took her seat in the middle of the hall, the first images rose on the screen, a rattling music sounded, soldiers marched off, girls and women waving handkerchiefs. Then the film strip tore, the electricity cut out. Now the war's here, Julika said.

Laci disappeared and Julika quartered in his small room. Men in uniform came every few days, searching for Ábel Stern, and Julika could say without lying that she'd never seen him. The uniformed men illuminated every corner of the cinema, ripped out entire seating rows, as if they suspected people of hiding in the floor; they stepped up to the wall cladding, yanked at the curtains, hit the projectors with their batons and rummaged in the rolls of film. A hot summer went by, a desolate autumn announced itself, and in early October Julika walked up to one of the projectors and said: The first town has been liberated. The projector sighed deeply. A few days later Laci and Julika stood at the outermost edge of the courtyard, by the bare walnut tree, and Laci told her about the films he projected in his mind while in hiding. He wore his handsome if somewhat greasy Borsalino hat and asked Julika to tell him everything she knew about the liberation of his hometown. Bullets zipped through the streets and one strayed into the courtyard and directly hit the nearly forgotten box of film remnants. Julika and Laci jumped back from the sudden burst of flames, but the Borsalino sailed aloft, spirited by the blast of air from the fire, and were it not for Julika's dauntless jump it might have burst into flames or floated off over the wall, singed, but she saved the hat, plucking it from the air, only now it had a cracked brim from the fire. Touched by her bravery and prowess, Laci promised to take her along with him, away from Budapest, to his hometown, which already lay in the radiance of freedom, surrounded by vastness and the horizon, waiting for him, wanting for a cinema.

It was winter and the ground was either frozen solid or muck up to the ankles, bridges across waterways were in pieces, farmsteads abandoned. On their way to the south-east, things occurred that Laci had always thought happened only in films: they beheaded gaunt, half-frozen chickens, slept in abandoned beds and slipped shoes off the dead in order to proceed with dry feet; they crouched in spindly bushes and watched military convoys pass, and they lost all sense of direction beneath a grey, sunless sky. Laci had to concede to Julika that landmarks visible over a long distance would have been of greater value in their situation than the horizon, blurring into the late-winter plain. They passed through the Russian checkpoints only thanks to Julika, who as it turned out was fluent in Russian and in addition could prove she belonged to an anti-fascist underground organization, which hatched its interventions disguised as a troupe of passionate artistic gymnasts.

In March they reached Laci's hometown, where it was cold and wet but already smelled of spring, and flying across the sky was a flock of large birds, which Julika described as cranes, and Laci took for crows. The door to his parents' house was unlocked, and for the first time Laci was happy they had passed away early. He walked through the village with Julika, pointing out the abandoned houses and names of the owners who would never return, as well as the house where the great poet Attila József had lived, whose eyes Laci claimed he could still remember, because they had glowed and sparkled, certainly without ever coming in contact with sparkling eyedrops. Attila József! Julika said. So Attila József had sparkling eyes—who would have thought.

Spring erupted overnight, as it does, and two days after the last ice had disappeared from the ponds the wild cherry trees bloomed and frogspawn dreamed in puddles illuminated by the sun. Laci, back home again, was greeted here and there as if he had returned from the kingdom of the dead, and before long he started working towards his vision, selecting the work shed on his parents' property for his future cinema. He cleared it out and swept up, while Julika, springing artfully into the air, used a besom to clear the cobwebs under the ceiling. Thanks to the support of a Russian delegation Julika had artfully enchanted, in autumn Laci was able to borrow a motorcycle with a trailer to pick up a projector from the dilapidated cinema in Hódmezővásárhely, where they proclaimed the death of the cinema. It was just the sort of day Laci had feared he would never experience again during his Budapest years: the sky smoke-blue with October mist, yet cloudless, the acacia leaves yellow and gently fluttering, and the ground, blanketed in stubble, was endless, flat, and so empty that it was possible to make out the curvature of the earth where the horizon met the sky, shimmering violet. The lanky man who unbarred the door, which was partially kicked-in, had a mocking air when he congratulated Laci and his helpers, who had followed him on a clattering motorcycle with a sidecar. It was a single, old-fashioned projector without casing, speckled by bird faeces. Laci suspected the pigeons which watched him from the open-air duct below the ceiling, their eyes sparkling with suspicion; they must have grown accustomed to the furnishings in their habitation and were outraged by the sudden dismantling. It smelled pungently of faeces and disintegrating film, which spilled out of a half-open tin, film strips scattered on the ground, surrounded by dead flies, which lay there as if mown down by the celluloid fumes. In addition to the projector, Laci also took the small cutting table, two loudspeakers and a pair of oddly well-preserved white cotton gloves, which he entrusted to the assistant in the sidecar once they had secured the projector to the trailer.

Winter came, more black-and-white than ever, with hungry birds dropping from the trees, clattering like toys, and people committed murder and manslaughter in the name of firewood. Julika grew at first restless, then melancholy, and when spring returned Laci sent her to Budapest for a film. Julika stayed away a long time. She returned, bringing sad news of a fire that had ravaged the Csillag Cinema, and a list of Russian films they could put their names in for. Laci wasn't familiar with any of them and finally, on Julika's advice, he decided on *By the Bluest of Seas*.

Laci dressed elegantly for the opening of his shed-and-wooden-bench cinema. Julika had stretched bed linens for a screen, and the projector was fuelled by a generator. Laci thanked the audience for coming and promised them that the future of the cinema was golden, and one day there would be upholstered seats and a real screen, a cinema *büfé* and a coat check. The first showing was free, but a small wooden shed waited at the entrance, through whose window Julika would sell tickets in the future.

No film could have been better suited for a region so eagerly defined by what it lacked, where the people expressed the absence of this and that—a coastline, among other things—in such exhaustive, polyphonic lamentations. As if lightheaded from the sight of the swaying boats and the undulating sea with all its dangers and attractions, after the programme the audience tottered outside where they believed they recognized the sea in the endless vastness looming at the end of every street in the evening twilight. No one spoke of anything but the blue sea from the film, quickly forgetting it had been black-and-white, and day after day, people streamed in, tired from work and tired from inactivity, baffled by the frequency of their cinema visits and the similarity between the surrounding landscape and the sea, recognizable whenever they left the cinema.

Laci was proud of their cinema's success, whereas Julika secretly wished to leave and sulkily began to prepare a garden where, as the next summer proved, only cucumbers would thrive—and in such profusion that she would line up against the wall of the shed-cinema an entire army of large, bulbous preserving jars covered by plates, where for weeks the cucumbers dreamt, fermenting in the murky liquid, as they transformed into pickles. In autumn, due to their overabundance, Julika sold them as a snack at the cinema, and in town and the environs they became nearly as famous as the film *By the Bluest of Seas*, laying the foundation for the town's first cinema *büfé*. Occasionally, on evenings without screenings, at dusk she sat with Laci beside the long squad of jars and sighed. If Laci didn't feel inclined to inquire, she would say: This severe grey twilight isn't for me.

That's not how the poem goes, Laci said.

I know, Julika replied.

Julika commuted between the lowlands and Budapest, mediating between the film hire service and Laci, between overdue notices and damage reports, conveying reprimands in the one direction and requests in the other, and organizing for Laci's cinema a screening of the first film from the new Hungary, which bore the appropriate title *Somewhere in Europe* and moved an exceeding number of viewers to tears, an event that touched Julika, causing her to further postpone her taking leave of Laci and the cinema. Just in time for the premiere of the film about the town's liberation by the Red Army, three rows of retractable seats were delivered, granted to Laci in recognition of his tireless efforts to support culture; the audience applauded, and the high officials occupied the first row of retractable seats, right in front of the screen, since no one would expect them to gaze past the heads of ordinary citizens. It was a very long film, leaving the high officials with a lasting crick in their necks, making them less well disposed to Laci's future requests. After the liberation film Julika departed, and Laci accompanied her to Budapest, where she intended to marry the official at the film hire service, to whom she had acted as a mediator for Laci for years. After their farewell, Laci walked through the streets of Budapest, jotting notes on the cinemas he saw, roaming the streets around the burned-out Csillag Cinema, where there was now a paint factory producing 'Csillag paint', a mural of a filmstrip on its newly built façade. The painted filmstrip showed a glamorous woman who wore a fur coat and smoked a cigarette. Through a crack in the gate to the open work yard Laci spied large, rectangular iron containers, something welling over the rims, which he recognized as a slew of intertwined filmstrips. For a while he took his impression for an odd illusion, undoubtedly influenced by his memories of the place, but later he learned that the former cinema's owner, who now went by the name of A. Csillag, had returned and was implementing a freshly acquired patent for producing a new kind of house paint that incorporated dissolved film strips, lending it a particular shine and extra durability. For a long time, Laci was preoccupied by the idea of films being turned into house paint, and he wondered if the images still found an expression in the brushstrokes, for example in a faint shimmer at twilight or certain shadows that intimated figures and barely perceptible movements. This relegation of images, plot, and space into something flat and rigid pained him and he felt disappointed by the gentleman who had readily entrusted him with the Csillag Cinema buildings.

On the tenth anniversary of the liberation a committee from the capital came to town. They took their places in Laci's cinema, sitting in the retractable seats reserved exclusively for high officials, and watched the liberation film, ordered for the umpteenth time, and afterwards one of them stepped before the audience and announced the construction of a municipal cinema with parquet flooring, a balcony and two boxes, designed to seat over four hundred, with a real projection screen. Laci was already appointed projectionist, since for the time being everything existed only on large sheets of paper, and with a certain sense of relief he faced the shuttering of his own cinema. Since Julika's departure, the cable orders had proved tedious and inconvenient, and the films he wanted didn't always arrive. The last film he showed in his cinema was *Carousel*, and even Julika came for the final screening, bringing along a jar of pickles, as a gift, and her fiancé, who in the meantime was employed by the main post office, and for fun she climbed back into the wooden shed and sold tickets. Laci assured everyone he didn't feel sad, only strange. He sat on the bench beside the shed and watched the pickles flying in dreamy slow-motion through the murky liquid and for the first time he asked himself whether a jar of floating pickles could be a likeness of the cosmos. Before long, he missed the films, but he became a regular at the cinema on the way to Szeged, and a few eventful years and countless meetings of the cultural council passed before a large municipal cinema actually stood at the main intersec-

tion in town, across from the most popular tavern. Curious bystand-
ers and children gathered around and pushed all the way inside the
cinema when the disassembled projectors arrived from Budapest
and the experts carried them up to the projection booth. In a long-
winded process they were mounted and at last tested, and in that
moment, tears welled in Laci's eyes, clouding his view of the first
images wavering across that immaculate projection screen. Equipped
with streamlined lettering that glowed in the dark, the real cinema
opened its gates. Laci was hoping for a splendid name, suggesting
Csillag himself early on, then Cinema of the Liberation, but in the
end the cultural council named it Alkotmány, prosaic and celebra-
tory at once: the Cinema of the Constitution, a name that was
immediately forgotten by all, and which appeared only on the seating charts where prices were also listed. At the inauguration Laci
held a speech in the auditorium, which was occupied down to the
last seat, and he had planned to talk about the names he proposed,
something along the lines of the cinema being both a star and a
liberator, but he was a man, not of words, but of moving images,
and he became tongue-tied, in the end saying only this: Long live
the cinema, since everyone has a right to see further.

IV.

No cute. *Nothing* cute.

—John Cassavetes

On the morning of 31 December, I left Budapest. Zoran, who regularly turned up around the cinema, offering advice and inquiring about the state of things, had recommended me Tibi, a driver for hire who owned a large van and had no regular clients. On a rainy day in early November I called on him in a road sinking in mud near the village entrance, and we agreed on a price, and he appeared punctually in Budapest, before daybreak. As we pulled out of the city the sun rose, a winter red, immersing the vast landscape maimed by autumn in orange light. As if forgotten by the sun, which grew ever brighter, this reddish light hung for a while yet between the reed stems that stood on the edge of marshy strips of terrain, awaiting the harvest. Tibi and I said little to one another; it wasn't until we reached the Tisza that he asked me if I was familiar with the poet Attila József. *Gentle, the farmstead and warm, the stall . . .* He recited a few lines from memory and then explained that he'd been required to learn them in school. The Tisza flowed placidly, barely perceptible, nothing of a whirl or a quickness, its smooth surface reflecting the bluish sky, and on either bank were bushes, forming thick, impenetrable-seeming protuberances. Tibi abruptly told me about an aerial cable car he'd recently seen in a hilly mining region of the country. He travelled to the area for a driving job, and that's when he saw the cable car. It hung motionless above a shuttered worksite that was still guarded by a man and his dogs, which threw themselves furiously at the bars of the gate when Tibi approached in order to inspect the cable car from close up. Small, angular, somewhat rusty wagons ascended a cable over the work yard, up to a pole towering at the crest of the hill. It was so beautiful, Tibi said, maybe even the most beautiful thing I've ever seen, he said. That cable car. A wonder of nature, in a way. At the local inn the waiter told me it might be running again the next day; everyone was waiting for it. It rained non-stop and I stayed at the inn for two days, hoping to see the cable car in motion. In the evenings a jukebox played in the taproom, repeating a sad song about the sea every few tracks; I liked that, too. A few guests came in the evening and stood at the bar, and it rained the entire time, the cable car unmoving. Later the woman behind the bar told me it'd been standing still for years. The woman sang along to the sad song about the sea and I got a feeling she wanted something from me, so I drove home. I wouldn't mind having a cable car like that around us, maybe it would be better than the old cinema. Tibi said it pensively, amicably, and I noted that his comment wasn't an affront against me and my plans for the cinema, but instead had simply spawned from his enchantment with a cable car over a disused worksite in a former mining area. I tried to picture the cable car, the boxy wagons over the low roofs of town, faintly rocking, slowly gliding, but going up to where? Who would be able to redress this lack, and how? Why not both? I asked Tibi. You can't have it all, he replied, shrugging his shoulders. All I'm saying is, if I had the choice, I would choose the cable car. From the cable car you would also have a view.

My new home smelled of smoke, emitted from the fireplaces not used in years. It was a mild day, almost spring-like, and the rural noise of the farm animals washed against my windows in waves: the excitement of chickens, geese, turkeys and pigs. In the afternoon the owner of the house, an old Serbian man named Tódor, turned up at my gate to welcome me. We had met before briefly, only once, and he wanted to tell me about the historical neighbourhood I now found myself in, listing all the street's previous inhabitants, who in the course of the past century had died, moved, fled, or been 'fetched away'. I lived on the Serbian side of the street, whereas the other side had once been Jewish; he raised his left hand, which was missing two-and-a-half fingers, and recited the names, counting with his right hand, and whenever he reached a missing finger and its remaining stump he fumbled in empty space, as if he had forgotten its loss. Holzer, Kallós, Dreissiger, Deutsch, he recited their names, and then started again from the beginning, since he had begun to doubt the order. Deutsch, he started over again, Kallós, Dreissiger... He stood lost in his memories; he must have been a child when these names were a reality in the street. Say, when will it snow? I asked, but even when I tried distracting him with the question for the second and third time, his train of thought was unbreakable. The stories of Olga and Tódor, the spirits of the many dead kept me company that first night, as the new year dawned below the stammering bang of fire-crackers and a few minutes of church bells.

I visited the cinema in the winter sunshine. The interior was cold and damp, although there had not yet been a single frost; with the sun so low in the sky, a sheer lack of sunbeams had invited in this cold capable of penetrating all the way to the bone. In this state, the damages wrought by years of oblivion were more apparent. In the

small booth behind the ticket counter and the adjoining room I saw
that the old linoleum had blistered and broken away from the edging. Below that, cracked concrete came to light. In the booth I found
a tin cash register and a few open rolls of tickets in various colours:
grey, red and green. Resting against the wall were the framed seating
charts, valid when the cinema closed. There were three price cate-
gories, whereby the front ten rows were, oddly enough, the most
expensive; the price could meanwhile be converted only into the
base metal coins that would soon be withdrawn from circulation,
those rattling tokens that no beggar would bend down for any more.
The two boxes were not listed; surely, they were reserved for
high-ranking guests who seldom came, since they were aware that
a visit to the cinema would dull, even tarnish, the lustre of their
authority, what with so many gazes distracted by the big screen. I sat
in seat number 12 in row 12, a symmetry I attempted to adhere to
in every cinema I visited. Here I was sitting in my own cinema, which
from all the damp cold smelled somewhat mouldy and squalid;
dreams had settled down to ferment in the cushions of inferior quality and arose at the slightest draft, along with vain hopes, the traces
of an overthrown habit, which had carried particles of life and left
them behind in this space. The low-standing winter sun cast a pale
light through the window of the exit corridor, while twilight reigned
in the auditorium. I tried to imagine who would have sat where,
back in the day, but could not picture anyone from town, not a single
person from those street scenes, neither a cyclist nor a walker, not
a yard gate abider or corner idler from this slow-motion theatre with
a view to the horizon would submit to my fantasy, although nearly
everyone I had spoken to about the cinema had their own memories
to share, their favourite films, their habits. Had they all really been

here, had they all really spent precious, important, unforgettable hours here? Or was it a kind of fairy tale they told themselves, now that the town was abruptly in focus, in order to congregate in some collective memory? Did they all suddenly catch wind of something significant that could touch their lives and immerse the past in a warmer light than what they enjoyed now, in this age that had left them behind?

There was a knock on the glass door to the street; Ljuba and József stood outside with a bottle of sweet Törley sparkling wine, to toast to the new year. We didn't find you at home, they said, and it gave me a strange feeling, 'at home'.

The three of us sat on cinema seats in the front row and toasted to one another and the wall, where a screen should hang again. The corpse of one that now lay on the stage before the main wall, half-unrolled, had to be taken away. Where to bring a deceased screen? Were there still small residues of images and scenes sticking to the edges of the holes and damaged spots? Ljuba rhapsodized about the Soviet films of her childhood and showed me the portraits of her favourite actors hanging in the long exit corridor, covered in dust and cobwebs. I had never heard, for instance, of Nadezhda Rumyant-seva, who was depicted blonde and smiling in the style of a 'little woman', photographed obliquely from above in that patronizing angle photographers once selected for all females, in order to see the women looking up at them. We have to form a plan, Józsi said. Write lists. Write down what's missing. What has to be done. First winter has to come and go, Ljuba said. First winter, then the cinema.

The days remained mild, nearly spring-like, with birds singing in the bare trees and cats roaming in search of prey. I cycled down the bumpy paths between the fields and sparse groves, where it smelled of soil and smoke, and not once did I see another person. On clear days on the eastern horizon a range of hills became apparent, on the other side of the border, in Romania, a mild precursor to the Carpathian Mountains, pale blue shadows that held out for only a few hours before blurring into the horizon like a short-lived dream. Dusk came early, giving way to darkness slowly, in small steps, during which time distances shifted and the most inconspicuous of things acquired weight in the flat landscape, as if to tell their own story. In this liminal light everything appeared almost unreal and at the same time was concrete in its presence. On still days I spent hours with my tripod and camera, taking long-exposure shots, and I wondered what might remain of this unreality, and whether it wasn't a magnified reality, after all. I had to wait to develop the film until the next time I went to a larger town. The exposed rolls bided in their cannisters like inaccessible secrets, and I caught myself imagining the images in an embryonic state, in the form of pickles, floating in an undefined space.

My neighbour Tódor came over every few days, bringing new stories about the former neighbourhood. His parents were kulaks and he boasted of past riches and property that was taken from his family, resting his hand on his brow all the while, as if by shading his eyes from the mild, low-standing winter sun he was able to look down the street, across the intersection where the pub was, beyond the dilapidated houses where Roma people lived and into the past, and in his gaze still lay hold of his ancestors' large estate. Once he reported that his father had even owned an automobile and let himself be chauffeured all the way to Timișoara and Subotica, real cities with urban amusements. Due to all this, as well as his missing finger

parts—victim of an industrial kitchen appliance—Tódor felt
cheated by life and reality. A vein of bitterness always ran through
his reminiscences, which for reasons I cannot explain I felt obliged
to listen to. Once he told me that the Serbians had not kept dogs to
watch over their houses, but peacocks, which would let out a piercing
squawk and fly up onto the ridges of their roofs whenever a stranger
approached. It sounded like a tall story, or at any rate a slip into the
fantastic that later turns out to be true. When will winter arrive?
I asked him every time, mindful of Ljuba's warning that the cinema
was on the agenda only after winter. Tódor then looked up, scruti-
nizing the sky, and said: Soon. Definitely soon. One morning a
pointed wind blew in from the north-east, and the sky was so overcast it never really became light. Tódor was waiting for me at the
gate when I left the cinema, where I went every day to move things
back and forth, performing these small ineffectual actions in the
face of a much larger chaos inching ever closer. Now I remember,
Tódor said cheerfully, and began again to list the names of the former
inhabitants: Deutsch, Dreissiger, Holzer, Kallós... He said the names
very slowly with shut eyes and a while passed before he noticed the
first snowflakes falling onto his hand with the severed counting
fingers; thin, tender small flakes that at first were barely perceptible
on the ground, but after three days of incessant snowfall they had
blanketed the town and landscape in such a thick layer that entire
residential streets were unrecognizable and the fields spread out like
a white, unmoving ocean where groves towered as stubby small
islands offering no promise of shelter. Now it was winter, and I understood what Ljuba meant—it was so cold that the lock to the cinema
door wouldn't even open. In front of their houses and gates, with a
great slowness the residents shovelled narrow tunnels in the snow,

which terminated at the next vacant house in a barrier of deep, untouched powder. In the evening when the snow that had melted, either underfoot or in the sun, began to freeze again, it was time to spread the day's ashes, and with each passing day the snow in front of the houses was thus dyed a deeper shade of grey, until it was nearly black. In this cold, starving birds dropped from the trees like forgotten toys, weary and frostbitten, and helpless wild animals, knowing how to put their hooves down so gently that only a trace remained, as if blown onto the surface, advanced into the gardens, where here and there was a brassica plant gone to flower.

Olga came over, enshrouded from head to toe in fur, with a photograph she'd come across in her house, and it seemed to me she'd been searching for proof of her time as the cinema *büfé* lady, as if she needed to convince herself of her own past. It was a small square photograph with a white border, a somewhat faded, yellowed black-and-white image, captured in such a sharp focus that the facial features of a young Olga and the boy beside her, easily identified as a left-wing, youthful Józsi, emerged with utmost clarity, as was common for old lenses attuned more to distance than to a surface sharpness that scarce a human eye is able to perceive. Olga and Józsi stood in winter clothes in front of a large cast-iron stove in the cinema foyer, and as far as I could tell, the angular pillars were the same; the entrance was recognizable in the background, while outside darkness reigned. A blurry figure, clad entirely in dark grey, flits dead-left out of the frame. My place is beside the celluloid, not on it, the projectionist Laci supposedly liked to say, and so he remained but a fleeing shadow in the few photographs that managed to capture him at all, a mystery figure in which you might discern anything you wanted or imagined.

Karli took the photograph with his old Russian camera—Olga still remembered it well, regretting that he naturally was not in it. She would keep looking, she announced, maybe more photographs would turn up.

The winter lasted three weeks. For three weeks all froze to the marrow. Then a wind arose and the blackbirds and great tits and the siskins chimed a different tone. They dove upon what the melting snow uncovered: partially consumed corncobs, rotten apples, last year's remaining grain. The fields were flooded with snowmelt, the dirt roads were a mire. The equipment that had stood its ground so consequently in the twilight of early winter days now began to take form only slowly. Despite the dark fields, the vastness was bright.

The snow melted, leaving behind a barren mud-land. The enchantment of a snow-covered landscape followed by a brief brightness when it thawed now gave way to disenchantment in the form of weeks-long, incessant mild rain. Admittedly the birdcalls multiplied, and there were even twilit hours when blackbirds timidly rehearsed, but in general, whether due to the difficult footing caused by thick mud, or the absence of brightness and light, life slowed down, and this slowness was occasionally mistakable for a universal rigidity. The soil adhered to one's shoes in thick clumps that never dried. Thus encrusted, my shoes stood on the veranda and even by the next day mud still clung to them, only the outer layer being dry, having eaten into every last fibre and pore of the leather. The landscape was black-and-white, with countless gradations of grey, and every colourful scarf fluttering from the neck of a cyclist in the distance, every hat in any colour aside from black or grey jumped out at the eye like a warning sign. The veiled horizon turned dark, and in that flat, bare landscape the field of vision narrowed such that you couldn't see past the nearest clump of trees, the nearest intersection, the nearest bar, for which no street wanted. The bar closest to my house had a blue, flickering sign, helping lost people find their way to the table and the counter, even in the dark. There were often fights that spilled into the streets, when the wintery non-earners asked to put their bills on their accounts after losing their last coins to the clattering, ringing slot machines. The barkeep refused the deferral and moved to throw out the supplicant, and this was proceeded by a grapple at the exit door, which should open only for a brief booting out, lest the interior lose a single degree of warmth, generated by people talking and cursing and pleading and fighting and lifting up and crashing down their beer steins. Every pane was fogged, but not a whiff of fresh air should reach the inside, to infer from the exchanges by the bar door. Excited by the upheaval of the dispute, the guard dog next door gave mouth and his alarm was chronicled by one dog's oesophagus after the other; the sonic equivalent of wildfire, which seized the entire village in pulsating circles, often rising and falling in waves until dawn. In the bright light of day only few dogs were to be seen in the village; they lay in the yards, half-sleeping, half-lurking, some in their hutches, most of them leashed or chained, and on winter days each one was concerned with its own field of vision and its own zone. During these nocturnal barking excesses, however, all such borders separating zones and territories were blurred, and the darkness was now what kept the dogs alive, and they emitted these hoarse, yapping, yelping, rumbling tones from their throats in unforeseen solidarity. It was the local night-song of the dogs. Perhaps it was the paralyzing lack of action and the uneventfulness of these February weeks that caused me to doubt all I had set out to do here. Even Józsi sat in silence beside the cast-iron stove in his bicycle shop, evading all conversation, not once mentioning the cinema. He patched and tinkered away in silence and got to work on old, defective sewing machines, since no one bought bicycles in winter, although the cycling traffic hadn't slowed down a bit, not even in the weeks of snow and ice. I once saw Olga set off for the shop, teetering on her bicycle, only to later also become witness to her crashing in the slush on her return trip; she seemed embarrassed by it, and she wanted to reject my help, yet she wasn't able to command her feet—stuck into the heavy, irregular, custom black shoes—and neatly place them side by side in order to straighten herself, stand up and walk away, to say nothing of lifting her heavy bicycle. I led her through the slush to her yard gate, brought her the bicycle and her purchases and then helped her into a seat in the cool dusk of her house, whose shutters she rarely opened. She seemed addled and disconcerted by her fall and sent me away with a mute wave.

Despite the barren mud-lands, I continued taking my walks and once even circled the entire town, which took a surprising length of time; yes, it even left me wondering if I had perhaps, lost in thought, taken a wrong turn somewhere and was now moving along the periphery of a different place altogether, but then I saw it, flickering at some distance away, already at the fall of dusk, the blue illuminated sign of the bar on my corner, and I considered myself saved.

Some days I felt like an extra in a film, standing at the outermost edge of a scene. György Fehér's *Passion* came to mind, or Béla Tarr's *Damnation*, and I now recognized truths there that had previously remained hidden to me. The rigidity and inertia that accompany thick mud, universal inaction and the undulations of barking dogs;

an entanglement in splintered hopes that hold no future; the aborted upkeep of a memory which no longer knows where the past begins; the neglect of providence in precisely this region, blessed with such vastness and so much horizon in other seasons and weather conditions. The great weariness of the person who has toiled to the bone beside an immense sky, and then, exhausted, falls asleep at the edge of the field below the burden of emptiness, and can feel the grass growing beneath their heart. At night I lay awake, listening in on the dogs or the seldom, barkless silence so thick and heavy with darkness, and I wondered what films I should and could screen here. I thought about the intoxicated film-spendthrift Cassavetes and his urban-attuned film distillate of doubt and alienation; I thought about Béla Tarr, about *Lola Montès*, *Alphaville* and *A Taste of Honey*, and in my imagination, I projected stills from these films on the main wall of the cinema. I took nocturnal notes in which for instance *Days of Heaven* or *Tokyo Story* always seemed to be the most innocuous options, but I always discarded them as soon as I considered the audience. It slowly dawned on me that I was practised only in seeing, and not in showing. Drained, in the end I was preoccupied only by the question of why Béla Tarr—in my memory, at least—had a moustache that I associated with Hungarian large-scale farmers from historical films. A moustache of kulaks and Huns, which had the effect of a displaced prop when I saw him onstage at the National Film Theatre by the River Thames in London. Was the moustache reality? Had I, after all, ascribed it to the director in my mind, and if so, why? When I awoke into yet another drizzling morning, this last whirligig of thought had been forgotten in restless sleep and, feeling determined, I continued to wonder what responsibility I bore as the mistress of a cinema, and I concluded that it could only be to reawaken a space for collective seeing. And eventually, after a night of dog-silence and owls hooting in the distance, the sun rose from a pale morning twilight. The rain had dried up.

Once again, out of a clear sky the frost bit in, causing the swells of mud to freeze overnight into rimy miniature mountain ranges, while the birds expelled sounds of alarm and a layer of ice covered the ponds and puddles. The cold snap lasted a few days, as if the spring needed this wintery leg-up, this performance of freeing the landscape from ice, lifting a curtain of hoarfrost in order to open the view to light, warmth, frogspawn and violet blossoms, the disposition for a new beginning stirring everywhere. A woman knocked on my window and introduced herself as Rozalia. I recognized her as the ice cream shop bicycle driver of last year. She was looking for work and offered her services as a cleaning woman. We walked over to the cinema, where she'd never been; she was the first person in town who didn't offer me her memories of the cinema as a welcome gift, whether of a certain film or her habits in connection with the place, *mozi*. She had never been inside a cinema in all her life, she said, shrugging her shoulders, without regret, and in the viewing room she asked me if such a great number of people had ever really come together, in order to watch something like television being projected up there, at the spot where a screen should be again someday. She asked her questions without wonder, and while walking through the rooms, all of which needed to be cleaned, she sometimes picked up an object and spun it around in her fingers—a small jar of ink on the table beside the ticket register, a brush at the coat check, a knife in the projection booth—but she asked nothing, and in general seemed utterly without curiosity. Where are you from, I asked her, and she replied, shrugging her shoulders: From here.

She lived nearby and it was convenient for her until the ice cream shop reopened and she would once again ride through the streets on the delivery bicycle. She also remained unaffected when we discovered a burst pipe in the rear part of the cinema—the reason for the distinct sound of rushing water that I'd taken for an illusion as we walked through the rooms. The water flowed unimpeded into the yard from one of the battered lavatories, as if the water stream had already undermined the masonry walls and forged a path. In my mind's eye I watched the rear wall above the developing cavity teeter and then collapse. I'd forgotten to turn off the water for winter: my first failure in my dealings with the *mozi*. Rozalia lost her composure only when she discovered, on our way to the front door, a photograph of Marcello Mastroianni lying on the coat-check counter. It once hung in the exit corridor across from the screening room, along with the other standard portraits in asymmetric picture frames with removable backs, a fixture reminiscent of the sixties, which could be used for a rotating exhibition of the stars of the hour. Spellbound, Rozalia stood in front of the framed photograph and carefully wiped the glass with the arm of her quilted jacket, removing a layer of dust, which would settle back down on the picture before long. I know this guy! She sighed enthusiastically, I definitely know him! Most definitely!

Rozalia came every day and devoted herself to the dusty and soiled photographs of actors, the colourful seating charts with ticket prices, which had changed in regular intervals throughout the years, and the other posters, signs and objects that we found in the closets and building additions. A short history of the cinema business came together, beginning with the first generation of cheap retractable seats and a heavy flashlight that Olga might have used when she left the *büfé*, in order to direct the latecomers to their seats in the auditorium, down to a magnificent certificate in a gold-coloured frame, which documented the *mozi* staff's first-place win at the socialist workers' competition of 1975. This discovery moved Rozalia nearly as much as her discovery of Marcello Mastroianni's photograph, in which she recognized the face of who-knows-whom. I was ten! she called out when the certificate emerged behind a stack of framed pictures, a call of wistfulness and astonishment, as if this long-past competition was a missed opportunity for her to prove her worth, and I had to promise that the certificate would hang in a prominent place once the cinema reopened. Rozalia cleaned every object with devotion, and rested the clean pictures against the walls side by side in the room behind the box office, as if preparing for an exhibition. Thus arranged, the photographs seemed like mass-produced goods: the repeated poses, the upturned gazes, be they studied or instructed, the uniform of attractiveness—whether an unbuttoned men's shirt or an embroidered peasant blouse—and the nuances of the smile, wavering between cheerful and melancholic, harmless and malicious, all once flawless templates, already in circulation long before there was photo-editing on screens. I knew the names of only a few of the portrayed. I had never seen them in the cinema, they awoke no memories; perhaps that was the reason I never found a view that allowed me to look past the two-dimensionality of the pictures, into a beyond. But here these faces and names had defined the screen; they had been alone with the viewers in the dark auditorium, they haunted their minds and were entwined in their pasts, offering models of cadence, of pitch, of voice, head positions, gestures and movements that I would not recognize, since I had never experienced them here and not even seen them on the screen at all. They matched the magnificent employee certificate, the small enamel ashtray set found in a back room, the cardboard tickets, the now-murky soda bottles, the décor of the cinema and coat check, the heavy imitation brocade curtains by the entrance and the *mozi* lettering. They had enlivened the space between the entrance and exit corridors, where the audience's gaze and the shaft of light from the projector mixed, forming the particles that would settle down in the viewers' every pore, filtering out whatever had found its way in from the world outside the cinema. These images and objects were the key to a space that would have seemed empty to me, had I gained access to it. There were no spectacles to help me decipher it all, but I could see, observe, look closely, wait. Wait and see. Yet I still had faint doubts about whether this cinema would ever again be a space where one could sit, look closely, see, wait and see, in order to learn something about what once took place here between the screen and the gaze. The consensus today was that everyone came from far away, from a world unaccustomed to the cinema gaze, all of them projectionists at their own screens, who chose the cinema as an exception, who were accustomed to seeing in their own private space, alone or with a few trusted fellow viewers. The cinema was always a place to which you brought your own solitude, but it used to be that you did so knowing you would take your place among other solitary people; you travelled to the cinema, hungry for film, and left sated, brushing against the outside world along the way. You were not your own projectionist, but rather you surrendered to the beam of light from the projector, operated by a foreign hand. You experienced, learned, immersed yourself, without performing a single hand movement to execute or initiate the presentation. You abandoned yourself to the place, in order to see.

I didn't quite know where to begin, while Rozalia attended to cleaning the small objects. Without a plan I began to brush out the seat cushions. As long as I was inside the cinema auditorium I could imagine the project succeeding, but in the evenings, when I sat in the yellow house, listening in on the dogs, the drunks, the owls or the wind and looking out at the impenetrable dark that filled the empty plains, the vision appeared increasingly insubstantial the more time and energy I invested by day. In the evenings I got down to work, making lists of films I could imagine screening here because I wanted to see them here, hoping it would strengthen my belief in the project's success. But in the morning, when the sun shone through the cherry trees onto my improvised desk, and beneath the street-facing windows I heard the scuffling footsteps of the corner loiterers and the elderly women, who always found an excuse to borrow, question or criticize something, I discarded them again. There were many reasons to discard them, for instance Cassavetes's remark: *If you look at life, everything is a movie.* The sentence had seemed almost banal to me in the past, but now, engaged in the cinema project, which was off to a faltering start, it seemed keen and lucid, a reminder that this was a question of seeing, of *how* to see, not what, and that the local *how* remained a mystery to me.

I had purchased a new, stable bicycle from Józsi and took a different long roundabout to the cinema every day; it was impossible to get lost in the grid of streets surrounded by empty space and empty space on all sides. Once at the edge of town towards the Romanian border I heard bitterns for the first time; they harmonized with the frogs and the quietly squawking water fowl in the reeds and it sounded like a concert, a studied performance of minimal music that caused me to stand still and listen. After a while my gaze fell on a small farmstead behind the pond closed in by rushes, from which the music came; I had not noticed the farm before. A small ranch house, surrounded by amassed wood, junk and equipment scrap, as was common on so many farms in the village outskirts, which might have felt they belonged, not to the village itself, but to the open country, giving them a certain right to wildness. Three people stood at the yard gate, staring in my direction, and when I lifted my hand timidly to greet them it appeared as if one of them also lifted their hand, holding a stone. Perhaps it was my imagination. Their dog leaned into the end of its chain with such fury that I became rigid with fear, although I meanwhile knew that in these streets even the most frenzied dog becomes timid and meek outside its territory, pulling its tail between its legs if you so much as bend down and pretend to reach for a stone to hurl at it. But where did this territory begin and end, after all? The pond with the bitterns, which continued to drone undisturbed, might have belonged to it; perhaps the three staring men also considered the minimal music their property. These men, presumably equipped with a stone for hurling, who stood in front of their farm surrounded by decommissioned things, and the clangorous pond represented two different kinds of relative wildness; the spring sun, which was already burning hot, pulled a whitish cloche overtop it all, and beneath it they grew entwined. Had I already seen something like this before in a film, perhaps one set in Nebraska—for me an entirely unfamiliar country, Nebraska, it sounded flat and vast and empty—or did this scene, which was just as foreign to me as Nebraska, transform into a film in my mind? *If you look at life, everything is a movie.* I climbed back onto my bicycle, anxious not to appear afraid or hurried, but not exactly sailing away in happiness, either, after this abrupt confrontation with the palpable reality of that existential question regarding the relationship between the cinema and life. I cycled over to the cinema, without finding an answer to this question or other ones, for example: Why did my mind go to the United States at that sight? Uncomfortable questions pertaining to clichés and putting things in boxes arose and remained open-ended. Was this not a scene virtually inscribed in the galled borderland and no-man's zones of Central Europe? I told no one about the episode, and it gradually faded beneath the remaining memory of the vibrating beats of the bitterns and their sonic assistants in the pond.

Curious people frequently came from the street into the cinema to watch Rozalia and me clean, have a look around, ask questions, reminisce, call out: It hasn't changed one bit! Or: But it used to be like this! Nearly every day I received a visit from a particular municipal employee, who claimed to work in the department of culture, for which reason he was interested in the planned programme. I heard him approach from far away, since his bicycle rattled and twittered like no other. He leaned it against the building and entered, as if he had come for an inspection, then proceeded to patter a while and nearly every time he departed urgently recommending the film about the Russian liberation of the town; it was an exciting and moving documentation, and he was personally acquainted with a few of the figures who appeared in it. *Felszabadulás!* From his mouth it sounded like a battle cry fit for an old Western, in which the 'redskins' spoke only an artificial broken

German or English, aside from this battle cry. After his little speech the cultural official climbed back onto his bicycle and rattled off. The liberation haunted my mind and occasionally I even dreamed short scenes in various coarse-grained grey tones, with helmeted men, their faces encrusted in dirt, crawling among the culms of the reeds below a great sky, pierced by the unpredictable lightning of damaged celluloid. And finally, after weeks of advertising by means of a poster in the *mozi* display box, two workers showed up: a brick-layer and his assistant. They looked at the rooms and agreed to take on the painting and repair work, as well as the organizing of a new screen. The bricklayer Antal had never been in such a large cinema before and he looked around, amazed. Who's going to come here? he asked—a justified question. Antal was from a town in the west and had moved to the lowlands, which he disdained, because here the government gave even the most hopeless bankrupt wretch enough money per child to buy one of the small houses that were already licked by the high groundwater, abandoned by people driven blind by hope, who in the past fifteen years had fled the lowlands for hillier regions. A lesson successfully imparted two-hundred-and-fifty years ago by Maria Theresa, who, using the same tactic, lured vexed inhabitants straight out of the Habsburg Empire and into the unpopular lowlands, where the Turk's boot print was still driven too deeply into the soil for the Hungarian people's liking. By his own description Antal was an unfortunate man, who after training as a bricklayer tried his hand unsuccessfully at various endeavours that promised financial gain. In the course of our acquaintance he entertained me with stories of illegal battery farms in the basements of pre-fab concrete panel buildings, roadwork in Germany and chauffeuring for pimps in Székesfehérvár. What can you do, he said

146

over and over again, What can you do, people got to live. Most recently he led a bar into bankruptcy. I never had time for the cinema, he said, and it almost sounded like a plea for sympathy. One afternoon he told me the sad story of his bankruptcy, as we sat in the backyard of the cinema, the wind grazing the early summer foliage of the walnut tree, where the owls slept; by then practically all the rooms had been painted, and only the main wall awaited as Antal's magnum opus, after Józsi's expert appraisal of the screen—being that it was utterly useless—proved true. For his ultimate failure before his descent into the Alföld, Antal told me, he had chosen a bar, deliberately located very close to a bus stop, where miners from the coal pit got on and off. There he could reel in the men who drank before work, to make going there more bearable, as well as those who drank after their shift, since they didn't want to go home. He had barely signed the lease before the unprofitable pits were closed. Antal, still furious, told me about his efforts to retain his last customers, who now were preoccupied only by the grief of unemployment: he hired a reasonably priced strip-tease troop from the nearest small town. The girls arrived in a taxi; it was winter, they wore fur coats, below which they were already naked. After all those years it was obvious that Antal still felt cheated: on the provisional stage the girls threw off their fur coats and then put them back on and demanded their pay. That's no way to treat men, Antal said sombrely, that wasn't what we'd agreed to. I realized that he actually believed his bar might have stood a chance, if only the girls had worn a little bit of clothing below their coats. In other words, this last attraction also went up in smoke, his debts remained, his humiliation was cemented, and he warned of what might be in store for me, should the cinema stagger into bankruptcy. Antal's stories became

engrained in my mind, they became images that unexpectedly called
up the driver Tibi's dream of the cable car so vividly that in the end
I was convinced Tibi had marvelled at the cable car wagons in no
other place than Antal's abandoned mining town. After a while I even
convinced myself that the bar with the jukebox in Tibi's memory
was Antal's bar, even if the timing was irreconcilable. Still, it was a
pleasant, comforting idea, to think that the stage of one person's
bitter experience could become a place of longing for someone else,
a stranger who lived in the same town, only a few streets away. I was
vaguely familiar, from train rides between Vienna and Budapest,
with the town where Antal had his bar, and years later I found myself
still looking out for the scene of his humiliation whenever it slowly
glided past the window of the train, until the view was obstructed:
when travelling to Budapest, by a forested knoll, and when travelling
to Vienna, by a terrain ravaged by an abandoned building project,
followed by pre-fab concrete panel buildings, and that is where the
actual city began. Judging by its appearance, it was a mining settlement constructed in the early forties and planned with a ruler in
hand, and by the time of my travels, after Antal's story took place,
it was fully occupied by Roma families. They had settled down in
the small abandoned houses, all identical, hanging their rugs over
the fences and lighting fires in the small gardens. It was always smoul-
dering somewhere at twilight and fuming on bright days, as
I observed from the train window. A weak, trembling small blaze
or a smoke sign to commemorate Antal's loss.

In May I travelled to Budapest with Józsi and Ljuba. Józsi had
tracked down a depot with spare parts for cinema projectors, located

in the eighth district. He had prepared diligently, writing lists and jotting down numbers, and he even brought along a drawing of the projector's motor, which he referred to as its powerhouse. We have to disclose everything, Józsi said, consumed by his mission to revive the projectors. In Budapest the lindens were in bloom, and the sight of the tram had never delighted me as much as it did on that day. At Blaha Lujza tér station there was a cluster of noise, dust from the street and exhaust, and at first, after months in the lowlands, the sheer speed of it all took my breath away, although Budapest never was a fast-paced city. We roamed the market, passed by familiar second-hand shops, strudel kiosks and entrances to the dark, half-subterranean wine cellars wafting something sour and rank. Beggars stopped us in our tracks; old women extolled bouquets of half-wilted lilies of the valley; drunken dalliers sang through the gaps in their teeth; men who ran small, narrow shops selling 'gypsy-disco' CDs stood without a customer in a cloud of electro Turkish-sounding music, chewing on toothpicks. In front of a glove shop two elderly ladies dressed in identical pale-pink pleated skirts sat fanning themselves, as if they were rehearsing for summer and, more-over, were waiting for someone to arrive who would whisk them away, along with their beautiful shop—to Király utca in the seventh district, for instance. The eighth district, Nyócker, as it was referred to in an animation from that same year, was no place for ladies with a glove shop. We struggled to find the spare-parts shop, a corrugated iron shanty located in the rearmost courtyard of a building at the end of the street. It was still cool there, as if the month of May, fra-grant with lindens, had not yet succeeded in finding its way into the courtyard. A calico cat rubbed against our legs, *háromszínű*, a lucky charm in white, black and reddish-brown. Józsi was spellbound by the shelves with various boxes and compartments, all of which contained spare parts for different projectors, screws, springs, reels, clamps, objects that appeared mysterious and auspicious to me, since they might help bring the *mozi* back to life and make it relevant again. József stepped out of his role as bicycle repairman and became the full-on projectionist of years past, gesticulating as he described the projectors as noble animals that were currently suffering a bit, and he impressed the young shop clerk with his unerring precision as he selected the necessary spare parts. The two most expensive objects—the projector bulbs, without which the images on film would never come to life—had to be ordered; a technician would come and get the projectors 'up-and-running again', as the young man said.

Ljuba deliberately wore something nice for the trip: a floor-length skirt that stirred up the many small pieces of trash and islands of spat sunflower seed shells on Népszínház utca, but she was unfazed—with eyes aglow she absorbed the urbanity and took pleasure in everything. I shuffled down the ring road, looking at cinema posters, toying with the idea of catching an early show for the mere pleasure of sitting in a functional cinema; I walked down the street where I had once lived and took the 78 trolleybus back to the train station. Józsi and Ljuba were tired from the city, nearly speechless after all that had occurred, their gazes so exhausted they had no energy left to take in what passed us by as we pulled out of the train station: the freight yard terrain, the massive brewery, the city's slow exhalation of buildings growing ever smaller, until finally it frayed into a green no-man's-land, a signal mast from the airport towering in the distance, and as the train passed by a farmstead which lay nestled at the foot of the railway embankment, where in winter on the furrowed ground a circus was quartered, I knew that we had left everything urban behind us and the towns along the tracks would grow increasingly rural. They both soon fell asleep, as the landscape glided past in the soft light of late afternoon, which cast even the pre-fab concrete panel buildings of Szolnok in a placatory warm sheen, directly before the Tisza River crossing. As was common in Eastern Europe, the blocks of apartment buildings encompassed entire garage settlements, a zone invariably dominated by men: small, second, happy-hour-homes for men in undershirts, with tools, perhaps a half-functional moped sitting around the garage, and in the evening light they sat on overturned beer crates outside in front of their garages, men in their small man's-world, briefly brushed by the gazes of people looking out from the train. We always drove particularly slow past this section, and I always wished it would come to a halt to give me more time to recognize additional features of garage land, but that never happened; the landscape outside was a film that kept moving, a film without a fable, the only actors being the light, the landscape and time. The eye was the projector and memory the auditorium.

On the day of our trip to Budapest, Olga passed away, as I later learned from Tódor. I hadn't noticed her absence; she went into hospital already the week before, after a fall, and never returned. My inattention made me feel ashamed. Now Olga would join the other ghosts of the street mentioned in Tódor's litany; assigned to one of his counting fingers or stumps, she would live on in the street, in good company with the other names—that is what I wished for her. But first she had to be buried. On the day of Olga's funeral, I saw the women of the street slowly cycling to the cemetery. In one hand they carried bouquets of flowers from their gardens, and in the other they clutched the handlebars of their bicycles all the tighter. They brought along sweet william, known as Turkish carnations in Hungarian, dog daisies, irises and freesias. After briefly hesitating I went to the cemetery myself, located not far from my house. At the lower end of my street, between the half-dilapidated Roma housing with pasteboard windows and scrap treasures in the yards, Kigyó utca—the 'snake street'—veered left, to the cemetery, making it the only crooked street in town. The municipal cemetery lay immense beneath the sun: a vast flat field of concrete-sealed graves bearing enamel photographs of the dead, which in part were already so eaten away by rust and the elements that you could no longer recognize the faces. The grave decorations consisted of artificial flower arrangements in various sizes, faded by the sun and occasionally nibbled at by straying hungry dogs. As I would later learn, municipal workers collected the flower arrangements once a year and burned them. Then a sticky black-brown cloud hung over the cemetery and one wished for a windstill. The burning of flower arrangements took place before All Saints' Day, when people laid out new arrangements and lit candles, so many candles that the cemeteries in the lowlands hovered like illuminated islands in the dark for two nights, absolved of all gravity. But now it was May, the arrangements were only half-spent, and from a distance I already saw small groups of elderly women with flower bouquets, as Olga's urn was lowered into a small grave. I kept my distance, observed the women eating cake after the lowering of the urn, since they, like Olga, were Serbs, and had the same customs as other Orthodox Christians; I thought about acquaintances from Bucharest who, years ago, as students, would visit the graveyard every day and join the burial parties for a bite of food.

I wandered across the cemetery, studying the names and facial features on the enamel photographs, looking to connect dots between those who shared a name, to recognize similarities between siblings. In addition to this municipal cemetery, the town had a Serbian cemetery, as well as a Romanian cemetery and a large Jewish cemetery that was locked; to get the key you had to pay a visit to no other than the cultural official who was pushing the film about the liberation on me with such insistence. The Jewish cemetery was almost always abandoned and quiet, lying separate from the other cemeteries, just before the town entrance. In summer the oriole draped it in sound, and once every few months it was blanketed in fresh swathes of mown grass, as if to illustrate the prayer for the dead. I was not able to find Laci Deutsch's grave there, despite the recurrence of his last name, found most frequently on sombre, expensive gravestones made of polished black stone. The last burial at the Jewish cemetery had taken place in 1976, a year after the *mozi* employees were awarded the gold-framed certificate confirming their first-place win in the socialist worker's competition. If you took all the cemeteries into account, you might end up with the impression that there were more graves in town than occupied houses. And there was still a lot of room in the municipal cemetery: a massive, empty acre prepared for future dead stretched to the north-west, offering neither a shadow nor shelter. For the first time I noticed a small bush at the opposite end of the cemetery, yet still within the bounds of the fence, an island of blooming hawthorn, which, as I now saw from close up, was intertwined with blackberry vines and gave shade to three graves: simple stones, with neither crosses, floral arrangements nor candles, without enamel photographs. Two bore the name Kallós, and between them the grave of Deutsch László, 1910 to 1989.

Among other things, Antal and Pista attended to the main wall, which according to Józsi's instructions should be spackled and painted smoothly enough to function as the projection surface. I had my doubts; my heart was set on a *silver screen*, which in my imagination formed its own memorial back-country, absorbing and saving fragments, becoming infused with a space that only the light of the projector could awaken. But we had no choice; there was no new projection screen to rustle up. Józsi spent all his free time in the projection booth, disassembling, cleaning, polishing and practicing hand movements in expectation of the technician from Budapest. Not until the projectors were *up-and-running* again could the main wall prove itself; only then would we see how the image unfolded and emerged in the depth.

Light fell through the side door of the auditorium, making the wall shine in a blinding white, standing out from all around it, foreign and sharp in comparison to everything else marked by the traces of time. Antal and Pista sat in the front row, playing the role of the privileged audience in their stained coveralls; they leaned back and their larynxes moved in unison as they drank from their beer bottles. Józsi stood on the balcony and said cheers to the entire auditorium, the three occupied seats and the three-hundred-and-fifty-three empty ones, and the new, smooth, blinding white main wall.

Pista was a shy, small man, who I always saw silently hungering for Rozalia with his gaze. He never said a word to me, but now

I watched him rise and build himself up in a way that signalled a question was coming. I don't understand, he began, and I could hear him struggle to repress a self-conscious stutter, I don't understand why you want to have a cinema here. It would have made a beautiful parking garage, very modern.

With you at the till! Antal called out, and I couldn't tell if he was agreeing with or mocking him.

The cinema as a parking garage. How many cars would it have accommodated? Ten? Twelve? And how many cars actually would have parked here? In this region that lacked everything but space, where most people owned only a bicycle, while others had an old Trabant or a Lada, and very few people owned a modern car, kept under lock and key behind a tall fence whenever it wasn't in use. But similar to Antal's theory about a motorway—he once suggested that if only there was a motorway connecting this place of slowness, consigned to empty space and the horizon, whose population had mostly headed out of the dust in the last fifteen years, to the next-biggest town, and then on to the county seat and from there to Budapest, then all the unemployed people would find jobs—Pista's question, which had cost him all his shy courage, now shed a merciless light on the mindset that kept people going here: Everything was a waiting game, waiting in the shadow of an absence, waiting while counting the vacancies and empty spaces, waiting for a utopia paved in concrete, furnished with the symbols of a world of progress, which could be bought at a price: alienation from the things that were already there, and from your own senses. The parking garage symbolized a world where the *how* of seeing had become definitively irrelevant, and so its venue had to be estranged in a brute act of transformation. Not torn down, but re-designated: an involuntary, sad memorial to the solitudes that had once found shelter here, and the gazes that had looked out into a different vastness.

But who would park their car here?

Who would see a film here? Pista retorted, without hesitation, as if he had memorized this exchange in his mind.

He probably comprehended better than I did that the purpose of a future *mozi* parking garage was not really about creating parking spaces in a region of emptiness as much as it was about documenting the end of something, the finality of a change that was related to the rejection of the volitional act of looking-this-way-and-not-another. *To look is an act of choice*, to quote John Berger. The disappearance of the cinematic site is inseparable from the infiltration of this volitional act of seeing, committed under the pretense of a larger selection, and relegated to the realm of the private, the small, the controllable. Withdrawn from the public, estranged from subversion.

The lindens withered, the poppies in the fields let go of their white petals, and Olga's niece came from Makó to clean the house and sell everything inside it: couples and entire families came every day with handcarts and after a brief haggling and paying with an expression of shame, they took away the furniture, feather duvets, dishes, and finally the bicycle. If someone took the accordion, I didn't see it happen; at some point I wanted to ask the niece about it, but she surely would have immediately assumed I wanted to have it, and she would have looked into it, she would have thought about it, and at the next opportunity named me a price, unbidden. The niece was a friendly woman who, along with nearly everyone else in the region, was certainly short on money, and I didn't want to give her false hope—and I most certainly did not want to buy the accordion; in the end the niece would have pushed the pointy shoes on me, too. Every morning the niece stood by the yard gate, squinting in the sun, be it in expectation of announced customers, be it in the hope of drawing the curiosity of vague acquaintances cycling past, potentially leading to a purchase. And so she also waved invitingly, yet in vain, to a musician who traversed the street with his guitar. I saw him constantly; he appeared to be something of a local celebrity—everywhere he went people waved and called out to him, yet most of the time it was in ridicule. He always brought along his guitar, painted red, carrying it under his arm or wearing it around his shoulder on a strap, and occasionally he would sing along at the top of his lungs in a voice that was bellowing, yet also sorrowful, and from a distance you might mistake it for a case of the hiccups. He always wore the same beret, and even on hot days he had on a blazer. Most of the time I took him for drunk; I would see him sitting by the road talking to himself or strumming his guitar beside the entrance to a bar, where drinkers gathered around and threw a few coins at his feet, or sometimes I saw him striking chords before the busted windows of small abandoned houses—then he would stand there, in the tall grass, one leg in front of the other, slightly bent, like a jester practicing to become a troubadour, for fun, yet not without affliction. I learned that his nickname was Bendzsó and eventually I figured out that this was the Hungarian word for banjo; perhaps people called him that because of his red guitar. He also showed up at the cinema a few times, yet he never came inside and never played there, just peered through the glass doors in curiosity, pressing his face against the pane like a child, the tip of his nose flattened and white. One day he came into the foyer and plucked a few strings. He heard the cinema was opening. Difficult to say if he was drunk. Rozalia and Pista laughed at him and made fun of his guitar, as those who have been badgered themselves are always quick to seize an opportunity to humiliate someone else. Encouraged by Rozalia's laughter, Pista even reached out to brush the strings, but Bendzsó was unexpectedly fleetfooted, kicking Pista in the shin—this, too, Rozalia found funny. Bendzsó explained that he wanted to play his guitar at the opening. His roots were in the cinema, so to speak, it was in his blood. He played a few chords and sang, a melancholic bellowing, the words barely intelligible. Bendzsó noticed my hesitation and reached into his jacket pocket and pulled out a few wrinkled newspaper clippings, all dealing with the actress Katalin Karády. A name I was vaguely familiar with, from films of the thirties, the forties; hardly a face to me, at most she was a voice from interwar chansons and seedy wartime sentimentalities. Bendzsó claimed he was her illegitimate son, who was born during the war, then handed over to foster parents and left there forever, while the singer and actress fell into disrepute under the communist regime and eventually emigrated. In those tabloid articles, now barely readable in places from being touched so often, certain things were underlined—insinuations, assumptions and speculations that Bendzsó quite obviously understood to be about him—and there was something there that he clearly wanted to appropriate, and it probably had absolutely nothing to do with the recent rehabilitation of Katalin Karády's reputation—as a righteous woman who had bought the freedom of numerous people on the bank of the Danube in Budapest during the war—or maybe he wanted to brush up against a shadow from far back in his childhood, or he simply wanted to see how long he could keep up a melancholic hoax and find willing listeners for his fantastic tales. Bendzsó wasn't mad when I didn't promise him an engagement. He left amicably and positioned himself in front of the cinema at the edge of the unpeopled street, laid out his newspaper clippings, as if he expected foot traffic there, and played his red guitar. He sang along. Police officers came out of the station and joked around; they knew him, of course, and had probably known him all their lives, but now they asked him his story, as if he were an unknown travelling performer just passing through, and he willingly offered them the slim narrative he had woven together from the gossip columns of old illustrated magazines. Then he began to sing a song that I identified, after I'd racked my brains a while, as 'Lili Marleen', the old German love song; he sang in Hungarian and in falsetto. An absurd little fractured comedy constructed from misaligned fragments of European history, with offshoots overseas, where an ostracized Katalin Karády had fled to in the fifties, was unfolding here, on this street in early summer, in the lowlands, in front of a cinema that was the object of an attempted revival; it was a shrill counter-piece to the searching lonely gazes found in the films of Márta Mészáros, which automatically came to my mind in connection with Bendzsó's story of his lost mother. Those images were black-and-white and gentle, always orbiting around the orphaned state. The orphaned state: that was the common denominator between Bendzsó and Márta Mészáros, despite all other discrepancies in tone and colour. Abandonment. Living in a state of extreme deprivation.

The technician from Budapest arrived, and Józsi left a proxy in charge of his bicycle shop, in order not to miss a single step of the repairing and refurbishing of the projectors. For two days they sat in the projection booth, drank beer and turned screws, tested things out, tweaked and adjusted the machines until a cone of light streamed from the first projector. Józsi pre-emptively taped together some of the salvageable celluloid remains that had been lying around the projection booth for years, forming a minutes-long strip, for a test run. Rozalia closed the doors to the foyer and exit corridor and shut the curtains; Pista and Antal sat in the first row and I was overhead on the balcony when the first images trembled on the main wall. At the sight of the moving images—two faces, a man and a woman: he was bitter, she was crying—tears rose to Józsi's eyes. Only a crackling murmur came from the speakers, but this seemed almost secondary in light of the images, which little by little actually allowed themselves to be centred and put into focus. Not once did it bother me that the strips were patched together; in silence scenes came to life, opening up a world. It was a great moment. Greater than I had imagined it would be and entirely independent from *what* appeared on the white surface during this first test run. All my doubts about our undertaking vanished at the sight of those images moving across the white, smoothly spackled main wall, which lived up to the task. At a blow the abandoned cinema auditorium became a dark room to which you wanted to entrust yourself, in order to look and see further, a cube of wonder with its own concept of time. My belief was reinstated: every effort to revive a cinema was worth it, regardless of where it was, and whatever parking-garage-dreams might be circulating there. Film needed this space, the screen, the audience in the dark, and the audience needed the dark, the anonymity under the spell of the images, the view into a filmic space that was possible only at the cinema. This was the only way film could come into its own. All eyes in the same direction, each gaze on its own horizon. Even the three in the front row appeared overwhelmed. Silent and awestruck, Antal and Pista admired the wall that they themselves had prepared, while Rozalia, who had just experienced a cinema in action for the first time, began to cry, moved by the force of what she felt she had been a part of.

The technician was spared the emotions; instead he was concerned, sceptical about the quality of the sound, and for good reason. When he inserted his own trial strips, the loudspeakers emitted nothing but a murmur broken by crackling. It was impossible to ignore the fact that you couldn't understand a thing, that the speakers emitted a murmur broken by crackling and not even the smartest accompanying musician, not even a worthy successor of Karli in possession of the latter's orphaned accordion from Olga's orphaned house would be capable of replacing the sound in a sound film. A complicated explanation followed, about modified sound tracks and new devices and replacement parts that would transform the sound track into the sound that belonged to and fit the image on the screen. The projectors were no longer equipped for the task, they had been out of commission for too long, the times had changed, the speakers were defective, something was missing—even here, a lack of something played a role, as it always does in this region. Something's always missing, Józsi said. Ljuba came with a bottle of sweet sparkling wine which felt out of place, but at least we could celebrate the images. After all, that's progress, Ljuba said. And progress counts.

The days were long and hot. In the fields the poppies were now dry and rattling, their heads shrunken down to dried-out capsules awaiting harvest. Every day a small storm brewed, occasionally only to blow past without effect. The cinema opening was scheduled for

24 June. A Saturday. A white night, Ljuba said, although there were no white nights at this latitude and longitude. Even in June the nights sank with an uncompromising gloom: the crickets chirred, nervous birds twittered in their sleep, the brief spell of the nightingale was long past. There was a provisional solution for the sound issue, and we ordered three films for the first two weeks. We spooked the owls whenever we sat on the back steps to the yard in the evening, drinking Törley sparkling wine. For twelve years they heard only occasional whispered dialogues from the police station and, aside from that, silence, save for the thin tones of small creatures. Twelve years without a cinema, Józsi said. Put like that, it doesn't sound so long, but in reality, it was an eternity. It's a world away.

The film reels were delivered in the mail, with each film in its own sealed iron box so heavy I couldn't carry it on my own. The postwoman was as strong as an Olympic shot-put champion, and among ourselves we referred to her as Tamara Press. Contrary to her unwritten professional code of conduct, she was always ready to help, and never missed the opportunity to say, with almost tender undertones, You guys and your *mozi*, before she asked about the films she was delivering, of which she was actually familiar with a few. Together with Tamara Press we hauled the boxes through the freshly painted, clean cinema and up the stairs to the projection booth, where the provisionally repaired wooden boxes with the sliding compartments waited for them.

We had rustled up a few rolls of simple numbered and perforated tickets, whose tough paper was nearly the same shade of green as the façade. The framed certificate attesting to the first-place win by the *mozi* employees at the socialist workers' contest of 1975 hung in the small box office so anyone who bought a ticket would be able to see it. The cleaned actor portraits in asymmetric frames once again hung in the exit corridor, where they sunk into invisibility at the first hint of dusk, since there were no lights there. A hygiene and safety officer came to inspect the toilets and the emergency exits and deemed them satisfactory. Rozalia was disappointed that she wouldn't be able to take over the *büfé*, since it would not be reopening, but she still would come for the opening film, she promised, as long as she could get out of her duties as ice cream shop driver.

Beams of a low evening sun fell through the foyer into the small *büfé*, immersing the room in stripes of light and dark. This light made it appear like a painting, in which somewhere, in a corner sinking in a deep Prussian blue, you might sense Olga's shadow.

On the day of the opening a humid heat weighed down the plain. The sky was of lead, not a wind stirred. We had hardly sold any tickets in advance, even though people came in constantly, asking about the programme and announcing that they would be there on the opening evening and also planned to bring along other visitors. An hour before the screening began, the first thunder sounded. It growled from far away, tinny as a thunder sheet, suggesting it might be a while before the storm arrived. Occasionally it also rolled past in the distance. The three of us stood invitingly at the entrance. Zoran glided past on his bicycle, waved at us and called out something that sounded congratulatory, but didn't stop. At the intersection youths rode their bicycles in circles, as they did every Saturday evening in summer, and a few pairs of lovers displayed themselves as well, the inamorata elegantly seated on the handlebars of the bicycle. Some cruised nearly all the way to the cinema, but then turned around. A wind arose, driving clouds of dust down the street, and on the pavement in front of the cinema small funnels of sand and discarded scraps of paper whirled. The southern sky edged nearer in a front of purple-brown, a twitch of heat-lightning running above the dark concentration of clouds. A young couple rushed over, perhaps afraid they might not get a spot. They bought two tickets and had their choice of seats. Antal came, as well as a woman from the floristry, who had dressed very elegantly, and finally Bendzsó arrived as well, in a jacket and a cap, bringing his guitar, too, although he promised not to play during the film. As soon as the doors shut, the first raindrops fell, and behind the houses on the other side of the intersection a thunderbolt pierced the descending darkness. Józsi went up to the projection booth, while I took my seat in the middle of the first balcony row, from where I saw the heads of my seeing companions, small islands in an ocean of seats.

Of the three films we had ordered, we chose *My Twentieth Century* by Ildikó Enyedi for the opening. It was a Hungarian film, poetic and clever, a film simply made for the screen, for gazing out of the dark. The decision was made, the film was running, the sound crackled and rustled and occasionally stumbled, but the images immediately drew the gaze into a world of strange displacements, doublings and wonder, sleepwalking with a touch of irony. The large cinema auditorium brimmed with the film, just as it should. Approximately fifteen minutes after the screening began, a crack of thunder came and the power cut out. Ljuba was ready with the flashlight, which cast a weak glow. Everyone aside from the young lovers went out to the foyer. The couple remained seated, as if frozen, or so they appeared to me, their gazes still set on the screen. Antal and Józsi stood at the entrance and looked out at the pouring rain, which drowned out all other sounds aside from an occasional gust of wind, the glowing ends of their cigarettes describing straight lines and curves. Antal asked when the real film was going to start. Bendzsó asked when his mother would perform. After a short while the lights turned back on, and everyone resumed their places, aside from Antal, who had taken advantage of the brief commotion when the power went back on, heading off in the pouring rain. He had seen enough of his successful main wall and likely enough of the cinema in general. Bendzsó held on until the second interruption, when he fell asleep, not even waking when his guitar, placed on the seat beside him, fell to the ground with a hollow clang.

It was a long evening interrupted by power outages, and once the film tore. In the dark pauses Ljuba guided us out of the auditorium with her flashlight, and we heard the thunder rolling in and out, the rain murmuring, and then it was suddenly over, the night was warm and sopping with humidity and brimming with the croaking of frogs, an undulating rise and fall in the dark. After the film ended the lights switched on, the audience rose and gave the film, Józsi, and the old *mozi* the applause they deserved; only the young lovers remained in their seats a while yet, cheek to cheek, by all appearances held there by a spell, staring at the extinguished main wall, and then they both stood up at once and began clapping, calling out: Bravo! Bravo! Waking Bendzsó. He picked up his guitar, struck a few chords and shouted: Long live the cinema! Józsi gave him a bottle of beer.

That first week we alternated screenings of *My Twentieth Century* with the other two films. Occasionally a few people came, sometimes no one did. After the show we sat on the steps to the backyard and looked up at the walnut tree. Józsi talked about Laci Deutsch. That man was a rock in the storm, he said again and again, never alluding to what in this instance was the storm. Not a week went by without Laci showing a new film. People always came around, sometimes only after the fact, to tell Laci that the film was terrible, that they wanted to see a Western again already, or a decent war film, or a musical, as in the old days. Laci was always friendly, he would nod in response to their requests, and eventually there would be a Western, or an old musical, but never a decent war film, only *Somewhere in Europe*, every year at least twice. Then they could count on the elderly and the ageing and a few youths to show up, who always looked forward to the film and would say: It's Europe-week again.

Józsi got his start lugging film rolls for Laci, and later he was allowed to join him in the projection booth, to watch him insert the spool, repair, rewind. The hand movements were actually more important for me than the films themselves, Józsi said. The feeling that all this life was on those strips, it filled the entire auditorium, so much world here where there was practically nothing at all. I always saw the image in the huge darkness, from the window in front of the projectors, and that's different than sitting in the auditorium, I think. But the celluloid never lets you go.

After two weeks we agreed to do three screenings a week, of two films. For two weeks I tried my luck with various titles that sounded promising for drawing an audience: Hungarian summer comedies, all inevitably set at Lake Balaton; an animation; a crime film; *Hot Fields* with Katalin Karády, the only film with her in it that we could get. And at last we also gave it a go with *Somewhere in Europe*. One of the Balaton comedies drew six tipsy youths, who were sent to their grandparents' in the lowlands for the summer holidays. They hooted and bellowed and sipped a sweet alcoholic drink from cans they had brought along and which they did not handle well. After

166

the movie I collected the empty cans from below the seats and felt relieved that none of them had turned sick to their stomach.

When *Hot Fields* was delivered, Józsi became so excited you might have thought the actress herself would emerge from the film rolls like a genie from a bottle. He glided over on his bicycle to Bendzsó's house and invited him to the first screening, but when the film ran, no one came—even Bendzsó's seat of honour remained empty. I wondered if the film had also run at Laci Deutsch's cinema. Bendzsó would have been a child back then, still utterly in the dark about his mythical connection to the cinema.

Somewhere in Europe was ultimately the *mozi*'s greatest success. A good dozen visitors came, even Antal with his wife, and no one was bothered that it was a terrible copy of the film, flashing with material scratches and stains. That was nice, Ljuba said afterwards. A real crowd. While cycling home I remembered it was a Perseids night; the sky was clear and dark, but as happened every August, I didn't see a single shooting star to wish upon. And what would I have wished for? For the *mozi* dream to hold out a while? That an audience would suddenly materialize, that the cinema as a place would be rediscovered, that fate would step in and catapult me back to a city with many cinemas?

After that I only ordered films that interested me, films I had always wanted to see, films I wanted to see again at last. I had my spot at the middle of the first balcony row and during the screening I quickly forgot the questions that otherwise preoccupied me; occasionally a viewer dozed below on the parquet, and later I found out that Józsi had offered his debtors, who were unable to pay for their bicycle repairs, the option to repay their debts gradually by purchasing cinema tickets.

The holidays came to an end and, as it is in so many places in Europe, September lay in the soft light of anticipated new beginnings, which would dissolve into the fog and wood smoke of autumn. But in September they gleam and first shimmer with a dizzying beauty, as if stepping forward out of the desolate summer heat that refined them. Józsi requested a film. His pick was *Leningrad Cowboys*. The sound rattled out of the ever-deteriorating speakers, which at the very least made the synchronization incomprehensible, but the film suited the projectionist Józsi, with his *Easy Rider* bicycle, as just occurred to me now.

Why doesn't anyone come to the cinema? I asked Józsi after the film. He could not have been the only one who still had memories connected to this film, the laughter of another time, mixed with dreams and hopes still in his mind.

Józsi shrugged his shoulders. Maybe people want to be alone with everything they miss. They sit at home, thinking about what they don't have. We used to have this cinema, it was here, it was a complete place. All around it many things were lacking, but the cinema was there. You held on to your seat, you laughed, and so did everyone else, and sometimes the women even cried—that's just how it is, that's what the films are there for. Some laugh, others cry—at different things of course. There's a fairy tale where the hero has to keep moving forward, and if he takes a look around, he dies or turns to stone. Maybe it's like that. Returning to the cinema here is like taking a look around in that fairy tale. Maybe they'd rather forget. I don't know. I really don't know.

Don't turn around, the plumpsack's going 'round, is a circle game from my childhood. I never knew what a plumpsack was. Maybe it's just the variety of past József was talking about, a past that you should turn your back on instead.

The drunks who staggered around the entrance to the basement bar across the street bellowed and whistled at us. They had a few insults to spare for everyone who left the *mozi*. After a shop selling cheap articles manufactured in China moved into the ground floor of the building, this basement room was all that remained of Karli's domain: a dismal, low space, narrow and deep like a pipe, with an old jukebox full of Hungarian popular songs with titles like 'Come Back', 'Don't Leave', 'Can You Still Remember Back Then', 'How Happy We Were', and so on. The drunken men sang along, full of yearning, an odd choir enraptured by sentimentalities of a legendary past, whose soft arms cradled everything that had been lost or gone astray, what was missing or thought to be missing. In late September we closed the cinema. József, Ljuba and I assured one another it was only for the winter, but we all secretly knew it wasn't about the frost, the snow, or a lack of heating. The cinema didn't work as a private amusement, the auditorium never filled with the magical threads spun by various gazes and an air of disconsolation always caught up with the large, rejected room and in the end, it became inconsolable. The inconsolability of the orphan. We packed the final films into the sheet-metal boxes and carried them to the yard gate, where I waited for the post van with Tamara Press. She was surprised there was no new film, but understood our reasons for taking a winter break. Stay warm, she said in parting.

We had gone through only part of the first roll of tickets, and I put them with the others that lay untouched in a drawer. I cleaned up, swept out, turned off the water and flipped off the breaker.

I adhered a sign to the door: Closed until further notice. Winter break.

What to do with myself? Where to set my gaze? While the evenings were still mild I sat on the veranda and watched the sky darken. Occasionally I climbed onto the landing of the rickety wooden stairs to the attic, from where I could see the sunset and the horizon. Against a beautiful, clear turquoise-to-orange sky, the village seemed like an illustration out of a picture book from my childhood, with its variously formed church steeples, the storks' nests and small clumps of trees beside low roofs dissolving in the waning light. I felt paralyzed and didn't know where to begin with myself, my time; something was missing, and I became frightened at the thought of being pulled into the vortex of emptiness and everything whirling around the absence. I worked my way through a volume of poems by Attila József, and when I realized I could not stay there I went to Deutsch László's grave. It was a shadowless day with a white sky, a beautiful matte autumn light, pervaded by the smell of the first woodstove fires when it turned cool. The open field between the municipal cemetery, which advanced slowly and systematically, and the thorn bush guarding the three isolated graves appeared larger and emptier to me than I had remembered them. I walked along the edge of the field, since I didn't want to stick out and, in the end, also be confronted; in the cemetery one always has to be prepared for curious looks and questions. Do you even have one of your own laid here to rest? a woman once asked me, as if only that would have entitled me to walk among the graves. I felt small and briefly pictured myself as a pilgrim. The graves of Laci Deutsch and his two companions were unkempt as always, with their cement seals and headstones, which would just barely cultivate a bit of gentle moss and white lichens. I pulled a note out of my pocket and stuck it into a small crack formed between the seal and the gravestone, as if it were the grave of a wonder rabbi, in Kraków or Nagykálló, for example. The folded edge of the note was lodged in the narrow crack, and the sheets of thin paper sticking out moved in the mild, barely perceptible wind, as if they were the wings of a white butterfly.

Ki látja meg, hogy már látszanak
kilógó nyelvünkön az igért utak,
hogy nincsen hiába semmi és a minden
nem siklott ki

Who can see the promised road
at the tip of our hanging tongues,
see that nothing is in vain, that all
was not lost

Two years after the *mozi* summer a buyer turned up for the cinema. A man with a bald patch and a bar of ill repute, located halfway to the Romanian border, where he had formerly also owned a dance club, which was forced to close a few years earlier—why, no one wanted to say. He had plans for the cinema: he wanted to turn it into a bowling alley, a decent place of amusement that would give the people something. During the viewing he already forged plans for the renovation and the radical disposal of all the *mozi*-fixtures, and he made no secret of his disdain for the crazy idea of reviving a cinema in this day and age. That should have been obvious from the beginning, he lectured me. More than a year had passed since I'd been inside, and in the months of neglect and inattention, a dampness had crept up into the walls: the paint bubbled and peeled off; it smelled of mould. Spiders had moved back in, adorning every corner. Outside in the yard the walnut tree dropped its leaves, as it was autumn, and I saw no sleeping owls. The yard was in the grips of a weed tall as man, which recently had spread widely in the lowlands and whose seeds, someone claimed, had escaped from a laboratory. The stalks were meaty and dark red and ended in umbels heavy with black berries, which the autumn was already beginning to gnaw at. No one had a name for this weed. I asked the prospective buyer if he knew what it was called. *Új gaz*, he said, shrugging his shoulders. A new weed. I watched him cut a path between the high stalks, taking big steps, as if to measure the distance in approximate metres, all the while muttering and waving his arms in all these gestures of malediction. Everything stood in his way. Only in the projection booth did he briefly lose his composure and drop his disdain when he saw the projectors. Sad as they now looked, after a brief revival pushed back into an imageless idle state, they still managed to provoke in him a state of marvel, and he touched them and knocked on them, two large grey animals whose names he didn't know, yet whose trust he would have liked to have gained somehow, that much was obvious, he would have been delighted if a warm muzzle would have suddenly stretched out to search for sugar in his pockets or his hand. Perhaps for want of a sugar cube he would have offered a small, pale base-metal coin of the kind they would soon remove from circulation entirely, since even a handful of these coins wouldn't get you anything any more, and it would have been a great satisfaction for him if the coins would have elicited a quiet, satisfied roar from the projector-creatures, a sound that might have vaguely reminded him of the snorting sounds from a television film with horses. He would have felt accepted and approved of. But the projectors didn't stir, they made not a sound, and the prospective buyer asked me what they might be worth, and how he could best find a buyer for them. The room smelled of chemicals and stale beer from a partly full bottle. Below the ceiling in a window hatch, whose glass was broken, a pigeon was perched, looking down with round, glimmering eyes. The amusement-business entrepreneur made an offer, which I accepted, and we scheduled an appointment with a solicitor. I visited Józsi at the bicycle shop and suggested he take from the cinema anything his heart desired. He shrugged his shoulders, embarrassed, and then nodded, Yeah, maybe. The poor *mozi*, he said, and I agreed. Ljuba was visiting her family in Kyiv, and I was happy to be spared another sweet Törley sparkling wine and her tears in the cinema that desolation had once again caught up with. I walked through the rooms alone, choosing the framed seating plans, the certificate from the socialist workers' competition, a film spool and a sign bearing the inscription *cinema*, since that was the Romanian word for *mozi*, one of the three languages of the town, where Serbians always claimed the leading role. Multilingualism was also accommodated for in the great days of the *mozi*, even if the Serbian word for cinema was not immortalized on a sign: *bioskop* would have stood there, a place for the show of life.

The days leading up to the closing passed grimly; it rained a lot, so the town sunk in mud and it was too hazy for views into the vastness. Now the town seemed so small, shrunken, as if it were retreating from the horizon and withdrawing inside itself. But on my last walk around I was once again staggered by the distance of the way; there was something chafing at the reality of time and space.

The bar around the corner from me had changed hands, now going by the name of Alibi, and ever since then, the sign—which stood out like a promise in the distance on this walk, too, confirming that I had at last returned to my point of departure—blinked with extreme haste in colourful letters, a small string of pearls incessantly travelling along its edge, and if you looked at it too long, you would get dizzy. It was still a homecoming symbol for me, even if I didn't feel very much at home there. Closing day arrived, and this time the signing of the contract took place in a law firm in an office building in the county seat, where the plastic furniture and the cheap rug were so new they still emitted some kind of fumes, which made my eyes swell and burn. The solicitor had to open a brand-new package of disposable pens for us to sign with. I agreed to have a coffee with the new owner, to seal the transaction, yet I didn't know what to say, as if suddenly he, his friendly wife and I no longer had any words in common.

My departure was not for another two days, and I went to the cemetery. I picked a gaunt little purple flower, a pale widow flower still blooming in front of Olga's house, and brought it to her grave, which I struggled to find among the other identical ones in its vicinity. Then I went to Deutsch László's grave. My butterfly-note was up and away, but I had brought along a small photo of the *mozi* that I'd cut from a contact sheet. I thought for a long time about which one to choose, until finally deciding on this one. It was not an interesting photo, showing only the steps leading up to the projection booth, and it was underexposed and somewhat bleary, at that, perhaps from a brief infiltration of light that occurred when I removed the exposed film. But at the top of the underexposed stairs a glimmer of light fell through a window in front of the door to the projection booth, casting it in an auspicious glow. As I bent down to stick the photograph in the crack, I saw something shimmering there: a small strip of celluloid, haggard and scratched, yet still recognizable as a film strip. *The celluloid never lets you go.* I slid the photo in beside it.

I departed on the first cold autumnal morning, a Monday; I took the early bus to Budapest, which left at 3.50 a.m. I walked through the quiet streets full of puddles, to the bus station by the river. Dogs barked in the darkness, yet without fury, and I wondered if they had become so accustomed to my footsteps that they kept from going wild. Small groups of workers already stood waiting in the yellowish light of the streetlamps—the commuters. I saw Rozalia standing among a group of women. She had changed, yet I couldn't say how. But, she assured me, she'd never been better. She covered her mouth with her hand as she spoke, as the women here often did, mostly when domestic quarrels had left a mark on their faces, or they were missing teeth. From Monday to Friday she worked in Székesfehérvár in the west. She was really lucky, she said. She found a job at one of the largest tile factories in the country and now was in charge of sweeping up the broken pieces. It's a good job, no evil surprises, she laughed, and I saw her maltreated face. You sweep up shards all day long? I asked her in disbelief, and she laughed, Yeah, so much gets broken.

I spent the entire ride looking out the window. A while passed before a bright strip became apparent above the eastern horizon. A very slow increase of light, with ever brighter greys seeping into the strips. Curious, how long the dawn is compared to the brevity of dusk. Perhaps the day didn't want to show and had to be outwitted each time anew, yet at evening always recognized an opportunity and seized the moment to quickly disappear into the dust. Once we reached the Tisza River a bit of pink and turquoise had blended into the strips, promising a bright day.

V. Epilogue

Csillagra akasztott homály!
'Twilight hangs there from a star.'

—ATTILA JÓZSEF

AFTER THE CINEMA SUMMER in the Hungarian lowlands, for sixteen years I watched cinemas die. They died in London, in Berlin, in Budapest and in Trieste and in Paris; some went quietly, others more loudly, some went quickly and others with a grinding slowness. They died due to lack of an audience, lack of renovations, due to the general rampant, feeble opinion that it's enough to watch digitalized images flicker across any old screen. The *what* triumphed over the *how*, and everyone became accustomed to having their own solitude, which formerly led them out to the cinema, instead to rest on the nape of their neck, their very own private little hunchback, which felt snug there. In a world that is forever growing more uncomfortable, quicker and harder-pressed, the illusory convenience of continually available data that yields a succession of images gave occasion for the intercession of the small gaze in the small room.

Sixteen years after the *mozi* summer, I travelled back to the site of the cinema. I wanted to find and record more images, to experience the vastness of the landscape once again and attempt to get to the bottom of what it was exactly about the aura of this empty space, what spell this region of deprivation and the absences in themselves had cast that allowed me to believe that precisely here, in this terrain of the eternal, slow film between the eye and the horizon, it might be possible to help a cinema back onto its feet—yes, to even turn it into an emblem for the great truth of the cinema. I wanted to see the multi-seated temple of moving images in its abandoned state again, to ask questions from the remove of years, either to myself or to the cinema auditorium, deserted as it was, and sound out the town's slumped promises once again, to listen out for signs of life, for the silence.

It was a bitterly cold day in late March. The train cars filled up at Keleti Station in Budapest. On the ride out of the city you can watch the districts fray on the impoverished eastern side of town. The poverty had been pushed out farther to the limits, it had grown stiff, and the former liveliness of the streets and yards once visible from the raised tracks had disappeared. The city was behind us, and through the dirty windows of the train car I now saw in the bright light below a thinly clouded sky, the brackish landscapes stiff with frost. I kept an eye out for the winter quarters of the small circus that I had observed years earlier on my travels between Budapest and the cinema town. I knew that they didn't exist any more—yes, the entire, somewhat dilapidated farm where the circus wagons and animal cages were kept in winter was gone; I had witnessed it vanish bit by bit beneath the asphalt when they built the highway, but now there was not even a single reference point left, not a tree, not a shrub, not an inconspicuous feature of the landscape, not a trace, that is how thoroughly the settlements of uniform houses, streets, factory farms and warehouses overran the no-man's-land of sloe-berry bushes, fruit trees coated in lichens, and the abandoned small

186

farms that were nevertheless gentle to my gaze. My fellow travellers did not look out their windows. They flipped through slim tabloids or occupied themselves with their phones and all seemed shaken by heavy colds and blew their noses regularly and loudly, and nibbled at snacks they'd brought along. The train does not stop once until Szolnok. The train station in Szolnok had not changed, nor had the 'socialist' tower blocks, the concrete panel buildings in faded tones of the sixties and seventies, which defined the city's silhouette. But the view to the Tisza, the bottomlands, the garage zone that belonged to the residential blocks and was frequented solely by men, which in earlier days you could study on the slow bridge-crossing over the Tisza River, was now disguised by noise barriers. I remembered scenes and images from my countless trips along this route. Groups of men and women harvesting the reddish-yellow reeds in the bottomlands along the river; a young couple on the train platform one 24 December, each holding the opposite side of a laundry basket with a newborn baby in it, the man also with a small Christmas tree jammed beneath his arm. Once, in summer, a woman and two girls with braids jumped together from the train onto the dusty soil, since there was no platform yet, only to disappear in metre-high sunflowers, headed for a village shimmering in a misty heat. The endless fields of sunflowers which transformed from green to yellow to a tired brown, letting their withered heads hang, parched, until the harvester came and seeds sprang willingly from the withered pates. Winter landscapes in an icy blue and spring meadows with wild larkspur and sage, stormy skies and cycling agricultural workers, an entire film of images, framed by the train windows, a film whose connection to the cinema town existed only in my life and my memories. Just as no two people understand exactly the same thing by a word, no two people see the same film from a train window. But now it was as if the view were misplaced, no one quoted Attila József at the sight of the river, and a line like *Gentle, the farmstead and warm, the stalls*, spoken aloud, would certainly alienate people. What pulled past outside did not seem to interest anyone: a late-winter backdrop in pale sunshine, fitted here and there with election campaign signs looking like awkwardly placed props. The brief spoken exchanges of my fellow passengers hung like lead in the air, about the food, about the time, about the distribution of bags when it came to exiting at the next station. This leadenness sunk deeper into my memory than any fleeting recognition of a distant landscape feature, or the light outside the bleary train window, or the whitish-blue sky.

For the last leg I had to board a bus which took an unfamiliar route. A late Saturday morning in a slow, lethargic country. A few guests had already gathered on the bar verandas, where the sun warmed them a bit, and as in earlier days there were also lonely drinkers who sat apart, staring at their bottles. Aside from this, no one was out between the houses, only crows drifting over the fields, but the streets were now smooth, repaired, and in this state of obsolescence the absence of potholes was more deceptive than the former bumpiness.

In the town itself little had changed, although perhaps there were even more abandoned houses slowly decaying beneath the weight of ivy vines and elderflower bushes, the last bits of paint peeling from the cracked window frames and yard gates, and in spring, when the late cold finally let off, stinging nettle would grow up around the masonry walls until it was tall as man. Despite the frost and the biting air, on this afternoon, too, the day labourers glided home on their bicycles from their work in the fields, skilfully balancing on their handlebars or their shoulders their tools: rakes, hoes and shovels. Occasionally someone walked to their yard gate, in order to look up and down the street, but no one lifted their hand to their brow to shade their gaze from the sun. Views into empty space, the horizon at the end of the street like an old, worn-out trick designed to create the illusion of possibilities. But for whom? Those who still lived here had forgotten how to consider the vastness; the magic I had found here years ago was gone.

I procrastinated going to the cinema, searching instead for old views and scenes, for a small spark in the surrounding setting, which would let a small vein of hope emerge, after all, in this land of deprivation. On the roundabout way to the cemetery I had to look awhile before I found the turnoff to the snaking road at the lower end of the street where I had lived, that's how greatly the terrain had changed. The houses where the Roma people had lived were either barricaded or torn down, the junkyard was levelled and emptied, and not a single person was outside; there was not a sound to be heard, not even dogs yapping. In the snaking road not a curtain stirred, unlike in earlier days, when every footstep awoke an irrepressible curiosity, a genuine voraciousness for new things, for a brief look at a face, a figure that did not belong in the street. Even this curiosity seemed to have disappeared. Lying on the cement-sealed graves were the same old artificial bouquets, bleached by the elements. I searched for Olga's grave and could not find it. The rows of nearly identical graves with cement paving had eaten a little bit further into the prepared yard, which nevertheless still looked massive in its emptiness. Dissecting the area between the rows of graves and the three isolated tombstones, one belonging to László Deutsch, was now a paved drive, leading from the country road to an elongated building in the distance, near the fish pond of back then, overgrown with reeds, where I had once seen beneath a layer of ice that formed overnight in a sudden cold snap, a dead heron gazing up at me blind through the ice. The low building found at the end of the road was evocative of animal husbandry; the hunger for meat here had remained bottomless. On the other side of the new road, at the outermost edge of the future graveyard, which no one was too keen on occupying, the three graves decayed beneath blackberry bushes and brushwood. I pushed aside a few vines to read the lettering and reassure myself. The name had not changed, the letters were blurred by moss and lichens, but they were still readable on the crude cement obelisk, which is known to be indestructible itself and will outlive every name. I searched my pocket for the stone I usually carried around with me, but felt nothing. Nor did I have a message for Laci Deutsch to stick in the yawning crack between the obelisk and the paving, as I had done back then. In this place, as it appeared to me, there was no longer even a 'promised road at the tip of our hanging tongues'; the only thing to hope for was that the path might end, that there would be a *no longer*, an unexpected fall over the edge of the horizon when it suddenly moved in on you.

The street where the cinema was located was deserted. The lettering had disappeared from the building façade, and the green was overpainted with a streaky yellowish beige wash in a hasty attempt to expunge, or at least a first go at it. The wood of the entrance doors and the frame of the display box on the masonry wall once intended for showing film stills and flattering photographs of famous female actors and male heartthrobs, seemed just as brittle and cracked as it was back then, and despite the cold, the wood oozed this familiar, unique childhood smell, which united all kinds of weather and seasons and had imprinted itself in my memory so strongly back then, the first time I touched the door.

A woman in a shapeless anorak awaited me. She handed me the key: I could stay as long as I liked. I was expecting emptiness, to find everything wasted, deteriorated; I had girded myself with lines by Attila József: 'The room/empty, abandoned. Sixteen years/have passed and I still cannot forget.' But I was fully unprepared for the view that opened up.

After several years, the building's owner had finally begun the great reconstruction. Open cement sacks lay around, paint cans stacked up, plaster was knocked off the walls in spots or had fallen off in patches. Everything was covered in a layer of cement dust. I knew from my former neighbour, the one who had organized the key transfer, that the future bowling-alley owner, whose renovations had single-handedly destroyed all he encountered, had died. Was it the effort, was it the pandemic, was it the horror of what he had wrought? I had thought to photograph the walnut trees in the yard, where owls used to sleep, taking off with a brief whir of their wings when dusk fell, or if they felt disturbed. The trees were cut down, the wood was carted off; from the stumps I could discern places where the saw had become stuck—perhaps the chain broke, and they had to replace it before having another go at the cut.

The interior seemed smaller to me than it had in the past, with not a single closet left intact, and the beautiful portraits of actors— old gifts from the Soviet Union and the former Czechoslovakia, from Poland and film studios in Hungary—which Rozalia had dusted and cleaned so meticulously, were leaning crookedly against the walls and a broken cabinet for film reels, clotted with spiderwebs and surrounded by the corpses of countless flies. It was a strange repetition of the sights from my first encounter with the cinema, only now there was no sense of hope. Another absence was all that remained, another void to consort with all the other voids of the region.

The greatest devastation of all had occurred in the auditorium— and it was not merely the intervention, itself, that shocked me, but the mysteriousness of its aim. All of the seating rows were ripped out of their anchoring, hoisted and repositioned such that they, one row close behind another, no longer faced the screen, but instead the wall to the right of it, where the open doors let in light from the long corridor, by which many years ago the audience had exited the auditorium, while in the foyer and at the coat check guests were already waiting for the next presentation. The people leaving were full of what they had seen, while the people in the foyer were full of suspense for what awaited them on the screen. The hall still had the same large, arched windows from before, comprised of tiny glass panes that let in no sun, and through a layer of grime I made out but a vague light and a few dark veins of creeping ivy, which had worked their way up to that height. At both ends of the hall, from certain angles you could glimpse out the window, which gaped open, either as a result of negligence or someone's weakness when operating the iron lever, revealing a piece of blue sky. Like this the seats now stood gazing away from the vastness; they were numbered as ever, yet appointed to blindness. Above all when seen from up on the balcony below the projection booth, they appeared like a herd of strange, foreign, confused small creatures that someone had corralled together down there, without a view, without a direction in which to set the gaze. The stage and the large projection surface behind it were left untouched, and I automatically imagined a film being projected on the sidelines for this sad herd of seats, since their necks can strain to the left only so far; wasted on tired ears, a promise which was ultimately futile. It was all that remained of the cinema, these empty, levered seats without a view. No direction in which the eye could see, let alone see further.

Appendix

The following quotes in translation are from Attila József's *Winter Night: Selected Poems* (1997), tr. John Bátki.

112 'This severe grey twilight isn't for me.' This line is from the poem 'Szürkület' (1934), translated into English as 'Dusk'.

171 The lines in Hungarian are from the poem 'Hét napja' (1924) or 'Seven Days'.

185 '*Csillagra akasztott homály!*' is taken from the poem 'Tiszazug' (1929).

191 'The room/empty, abandoned. Sixteen years/have passed and I still cannot forget.' These lines are from the poem 'Ajtót nyitok' (1935) or 'I Open a Door'.

Acknowledgments

Thank you for walking, looking, talking, reading: Zsófia Bán, Neriman Bayram, Sonja vom Brocke, Zoltan Dányi, Sebastian Guggolz, Timea Tankó.

ESTHER KINSKY grew up by the river Rhine and lived in London for twelve years. She is the author of six volumes of poetry; five previous novels (*Summer Resort, Banatsko, River, Grove, Rombo*); numerous essays on language, poetry, and translation; and three children's books. She has translated many notable English (John Clare, Henry David Thoreau, Iain Sinclair) and Polish (Joanna Bator, Miron Białoszewski, Magdalena Tulli) authors into German. Both *River* and *Grove* won numerous literary prizes in Germany. Her novel *Rombo* is also published by New York Review Books..

CAROLINE SCHMIDT was born in Princeton, New Jersey. She translated Esther Kinsky's novels *Rombo* and *Grove*, which was shortlisted for the Oxford-Weidenfeld Prize, and has translated poetry by Friederike Mayröcker, and art historical essays, museum catalogues, and exhibition texts for Albertina in Vienna and Pinakothek der Moderne in Munich. She lives in Berlin.